APOLLO GRANT

REY NICHOLS

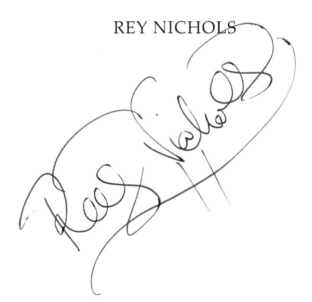

MOCHA MEMOIRS PRESS

ISBN: 978-1-7371320-4-2

Cover Art by Maya Preisler

Editor: Misty Massey

Proofreader: Nicole Givens Kurtz

Publisher: Mocha Memoirs Press

OTHER MOCHA MEMOIRS FANTASY TITLES

Avast! Ye Airships edited by Rie Sheridan Rose

Sisters of the Wild Sage: A Weird Western Collection by Nicole Givens Kurtz

Rie Tales: A Short Story Collection by Rie Sheridan Rose

Ghosts, Gears, and Grimoires edited by Rie Sheridan Rose

For my father, James Clifford Storch, who laughed at a piece of cheese.

All we need is blackjack and hookers, right? That's what my best friend Ronald used to say when he was alive.

Standing next to an unused slot machine, I wondered how much truth his words held. Scantily clad women wearing nothing but corsets and fishnets danced on blackjack tables in front of me, and I realized the party would continue if the tables and dancers were removed. Perhaps because I was grumpy, or because I had too much to drink, or maybe not *enough* to drink—I had become desensitized to the bells and whistles of the 24/7 Las Vegas nightlife. Looking around the casino, I found myself quickly becoming bored.

My phone rang.

"Hello?"

"Apollo Grant? Where in the nine-blazes-of-hell are you?" a man said.

"Murray, I'm in Paris." I wasn't lying, not entirely. A giant model of the Eiffel Tower through the window faced the street in front of the Paris Las Vegas Hotel and

Casino from where I stood. I scrolled through my phone and sent Murray pictures I took earlier in the evening of the tower, and the casino's ceiling which imitated the Parisian skyline.

"There's no time for you to be cute. Have you found the doctor's son?" Murray's grumpy mood made his tone harsh.

"Nope, but I'm sure it won't be long."

"Ugh. We spent too long tracking this one."

"Yeah, I know, I know. I'll call you back later." I hung up and slid the phone back into my pocket. To be honest, I had already spotted the target, I just liked making Murray panic.

A woman with blond hair, wearing a very tight-fitting red dress, sat at a slot machine two rows down from where I stood. Her companion, a dark-haired Caucasian male too oblivious to know the woman was out of his league, approached her from behind. He wore the standard t-shirt and blue jeans grunge look favored by college students who often came to Vegas on vacation.

I watched as the woman stood without complaint and followed her companion toward the back of the casino into a hallway which connected the Paris with the next hotel over.

It wouldn't bode well if my target got away. Not at all. They paused at the elevator doors and entered when it opened.

I picked the wrong day to wear leather pants.

I weaved my way through the crowded floor toward them. I'd catch hell if this mission failed.

The elevator began to close as I approached, but I managed to get a hand in the seam before it shut all the way. I hurried inside and turned, facing the doors. The couple didn't pay me any heed, wasting no time in reenacting the lyrics to *Love in an Elevator*. I waited until the door closed, and when it began moving, I turned toward them. Neither seemed to care I watched. The three of us were the only people inside.

I coughed.

The lanky man looked up at me. "Dude, what the hell? Can't you see we're busy?"

"I'm not blind. But I don't think she's worth your trouble," I said.

"You on something, man?"

"I wish, but I need a clear head for what's about to happen. You should back away from the girl."

"I don't know, man. You're nuts."

Tired of arguing, I grabbed the woman off her temporary boyfriend. Her response? Backhanding me right into the emergency stop key.

Fuck, that hurt.

We halted.

"Holy shit!" The man exclaimed, grabbing the nearby wall railing.

I knew without looking what shocked him wasn't the woman slinging around someone twice her frame, but rather the change apparent on her face.

Twisted facial features? Check.

Veins visible on paler than normal skin? Check.

Extra fanged teeth not present earlier? Check.

Baring her fangs, she hissed and dived at me. I rolled to one side, taking out the stake I kept hidden in my jacket. She fell forward, landing on her hands before turning her head and hissing at me again. I drove the stake straight into her heart through her back before she had a chance to react, and she burst into dust. Ashes from the now dead vampire fell. Whoever ended up in charge of cleaning the elevators next would be annoyed.

I looked at the man, brushing the dust off of my jacket. Murray was going to be pissed for getting it dirty. My previous experience with vampire hunting has proven leather is a bitch to clean. The wanna-be-boyfriend stood backed in the corner, cowering with his arms over his face. I slid the stake back in my jacket.

"No, no, no, no, no…" he repeated to himself as he buried his face in his hands.

"Get a grip on yourself, kid. You're acting like you've never seen a vampire."

He lowered his hands and looked at me dumbfounded. Of course, he had never seen a vampire before. The growing confusion spreading across his face spoke volumes. To the general public in this city, things going bump in the night were prostitutes and gigolos, not actual monsters.

"You heard me right," I said. "Vampires are real and they sent one from the Coven after you." Leave it to a band of local Vegas vampires to come up with the most unoriginal name for their group.

"She was going to kill me?" he asked. "I thought we were—"

"Going to have the best sex of your life? Maybe. Regardless, they wanted you dead, and I'm trying to prevent that."

I turned the emergency key, and we resumed our climb upward. I pivoted back around. "What's your name, kid?" I had at least a good ten years on this guy.

"Connor…Connor Griffin," he said, "and I'm not a kid. I'm twenty."

Shit. Now it made sense when I looked at the surveillance photos earlier why vampires were after Connor.

"Look, Connor, my name is Apollo. I would say I'm pleased to meet you, but I'm not."

"Rude," Connor said. We arrived at his floor and stepped out into the hallway. He huffed as he kept a brisk pace ahead of me. "Why are you following me?"

"Because Connor, I'm not the only one looking for your father, and if more of those monsters get to you, it will make my life extremely hard." A maid walked by and smiled as she pushed her cart full of cleaning supplies and fresh linens down the hallway.

"My father is—"

"Dr. Clarence Griffin, I know," I interrupted. "He went missing last year, and I've been trying to find him."

"Why?" Connor said, taking a key card out of his jeans back pocket once we approached his hotel room.

Something didn't feel quite right. I reached for Connor's wrist, stopping him from opening the door.

"Wait."

"Excuse me?"

"I said, wait." My instincts kicked into overdrive. Something lurked on the other side of the door. I took the keycard from Connor and handed him the other stake from my jacket.

"What am I supposed to do with this?" Connor asked.

"Pointy end goes in the bad guy."

Motioning for him to stay behind me, I unlocked the door and entered Connor's hotel room.

A foul smell instantly assaulted my nostrils. The odor was worse than the time sewer refuse backed up in the bathroom of Murray's apartment the day after that one Taco Tuesday.

"Ugh…" Connor said.

"Shh…"

At first glance, the room appeared clean. A king-sized bed in the center of the room sat freshly made and the curtains were pulled back and gave a fantastic view of the Strip. For a college-aged kid looking to have a good time in Sin City, the room was remarkably tidy.

Something dripped on my forehead. I looked up and found the source of the stench. A large circle of vampire blood had been painted on the ceiling.

"Shit, help!" Connor screamed from behind.

I spun around and saw the maid dragging Connor by his hair out into the hallway. Her face twisted into one reminiscent of the woman from my previous encounter. He flailed about, trying desperately to hit the maid-vamp with the stake, but failed.

I reached for my stake, and the maid-vamp smiled at me. When vampires smile, it's often unsettling. An uncontrollable shiver ran down my spine.

"No!" I shouted.

The maid-vamp snapped Connor's neck before I got to the doorway. He fell to the ground, and the vamp shoved the stake into Connor before running away in a blur of speed so fast, I had no desire to chase after. I knelt next to Connor's dead body in the hallway and pulled out the stake.

A few curious onlookers peeked their heads out of their hotel rooms. All they saw was me, blood dripping off of a sharp wooden object, standing over a dead body.

It could be worse.

I heard a click and felt a gun pointed at the back of my head. I grimaced at the fact someone—probably a vampire—had set me up. It wasn't the first time my lack of foresight had gotten me into a trap.

"Las Vegas PD! Drop the weapon and put your hands in the air!" the officer behind me shouted.

Yep, I'm being set up.

"Hey, now it's a party!" I said as I complied with the officer's instructions.

"Shut up, asshole! On the ground! Now!"

I didn't have time to explain the situation, and I didn't have time to be arrested. The officer grabbed my left wrist, pulling my arm behind me—a mistake on his part. As soon as he pulled my arm back, I pivoted on my knees and delivered a right hook connecting with the left side of his jaw, knocking him into the hallway wall. Onlookers gasped when the officer slid to the floor, unconscious.

"Sorry officer, I don't have an issue with law enforcement. You see, I also happen to be a peace-keeper of sorts."

I crawled over and relieved the officer of his gun and his backup, then tucked them into the waist of my pants.

I stood, taking advantage of everyone's stunned silence. Perhaps it was my six-foot-tall frame, or my brown hair and blue eyes on a chiseled-chin face which drew their attention. No, that wasn't right, the reason they held me in awe was because I made these pants look good. I made my exit down the emergency stairs. I needed to get back to Murray as soon as possible. It had nothing to do with the potential for being caught. There would be more of a reckoning for getting vampire dust on the jacket than for discovering I had been seen in public with a dead body. I could only imagine his reaction when I tell him the dead body in question formerly belonged to Connor Griffin.

Dawn started to break by the time I made it back home. The apartment was located on the second floor of a small building owned by Murray's family. A pawn shop called Queen's Pawn comprised the first floor.

The apartment was dark when I entered. *Great, maybe Murray won't notice the jacket.* I heard the sound of the wall clock ticking in the living room. Murray would be asleep by now. I just needed to make it to the couch…

"Seriously, what the hell, man?" Murray asked.

"Morning, Reginald," I said.

Murray stood in the doorway of his bedroom as I plopped on the couch. His ruffled hair and t-shirt told me he had recently awoken. I laughed as I watched his face sour. He hated being called by his first name.

"I was wondering when you were going to show up. You want to tell me what happened at the Paris?" Murray stumbled into the kitchen and opened up a cabinet. "Shit, we're out of coffee."

"Check another cabinet." I nestled into the couch, placed my hands behind my head and propped my feet up on the coffee table. I yawned. Hunting vampires and the like meant keeping a nocturnal schedule, and I was tired.

Murray sneered. "C'mon Grant. It was all over the news. 'Son of esteemed Osiris lab pathologist found dead in hotel'. What the hell happened in there? Security footage from the Paris has your beautiful mug all over it, even after I hacked in and scrubbed the vampire fights out." Murray took a seat in the leather recliner opposite the couch.

I shrugged my shoulders. "Who knows? I found the kid, killed a lady vamp, then shit went south."

"Maybe the intel we got was a trap?" Murray ran a

hand through his hair. "You owe me a new jacket by the way. Vamp dust is hard as hell to clean."

So much for not noticing the jacket. I smiled at Murray; he shook his head in disgust. This would be the third jacket I've borrowed that's been ruined hunting denizens of the underworld.

"I'll pay you for the jacket." I might have been lying, and Murray knew it.

"Like our jobs actually pay us money."

I laughed. "Sometimes they do."

"Pfft, whatever. We only get to stay here because my family owns the building." Murray rolled his eyes.

"Okay, so what's next?" I asked.

Murray stood and stretched. "What's next, is you lay low while I work today on making any of your legal issues from last night disappear." This is what he did best, using his technological skills to keep the law off my ass so I could continue saving the world and keep it safe from the big, bad nasties of evil. We made the best team.

"As long as you can get it done by sundown, I need to find out more about this kid, and why these vamps were trying to bait me out." I yawned the last word. I needed to get some sleep.

"Dude, it's simple. They don't know where the professor is any more than we do."

"Right, but I'm starting to think they needed me out of the way. If you get some time, can you look into why? If they are looking for Dr. Griffin, wouldn't it make more sense to keep his son, alive?"

"Yeah, sure. Apollo, go sleep in your bed, you're getting vamp dust all over the living room. I swear, you're the worst roommate."

"Admit it, you love having me around," I quipped.

Murray snorted in response as I got up from the couch. I headed past the kitchen toward the hallway.

The door to his room opened wide, and a voluptuous raven-haired woman with sapphire pools for eyes, wearing one of Murray's Queen t-shirts, stared straight at me. I couldn't help but notice the shirt barely hung past her waist, and her underwear had some kind of generic flower print on it.

"Apollo."

"Madison."

Madison Lily had a slight bounce to her walk as she went over to Murray. "Babe, please come back to bed. It's early," she cooed.

Turning back, I watched as Madison softly kissed the side of Murray's neck. She led him by one arm back to his bedroom and the door slammed behind them. I wasn't going to sleep anytime soon; the walls of the apartment were paper thin.

I shook my head. How Murray ended up in a relationship with a Vegas showgirl was beyond my comprehension. The typical computer nerd— tall, slim-built, and not entirely unattractive by a woman's standard—it baffled me why Madison hung around him. Hot chicks typically didn't go for guys like Murray. They just didn't.

Especially girls like Madison. I was the one who saved her from a vamp in an alley off the Strip, and yet Murray is the one who landed the girl? How the hell did that happen?

I went into my bedroom. The décor in the room hadn't been changed quite some time. Maybe because I technically didn't own much of anything in it, save for a small picture frame sitting on the dresser, some clothing hanging in the closet, and my stash of weapons tucked away in a bag on the closet floor. The furniture had belonged to the room's previous occupant.

I landed face first into the comforts of the mattress. I didn't bother to change clothes. The sweet embrace of sleep beckoned to me. As I drifted off to sleep, I wondered, how many years has it been since Ronald died?

2

I woke up feeling worse than the time my guts decided to end their relationship with a bottle of Jose Cuervo in the Flamingo's parking deck. You'd think I'd be used to sleeping during the day by now. Perhaps I should invest in some black-out curtains. Rolling over, sleep started its welcome embrace, and I forgot about my upset stomach.

Then, the alarm clock turned on. I couldn't think of a sound more nauseating.

Haphazardly flailing an arm out to the nightstand, flapping the appendage like a beached whale, I eventually managed to turn the damn thing off. Or maybe I managed to hit the snooze button. Hell, perhaps I broke it. Wouldn't that have been a blessing? Ten minutes later, the siren alarm blared again. I failed in hitting the snooze button a second time. Frustrated, I grabbed the clock and tossed it to the far side of the room. I'm pretty sure the sound of it shattering into little bits meant I broke the villainous device. It wouldn't have been the first time. This is why I have—rather, did—an actual alarm clock, instead of using the alarm settings on my phone. Not like I ruined another jacket. Murray needed time to simmer down after last night.

Speaking of which, I woke up wearing the jacket. I yawned, took the jacket off and hung it on one of the bedposts. I wrinkled my nose.

The odorous aroma permeating the room came from me. Gross. I stretched my neck and got out of bed. Stripping out of my clothes, I breathed a sigh of relief. And yes, I did strip. How else do you get out of a pair of leather pants you wore all night after fighting vampires and fall asleep in?

You're damn right I pretended they were assless chaps.

Watch out ladies, I'm a sexy beast. I laughed. Maybe if I keep telling myself that, it'll become true one day. *I need to get laid.*

I stumbled naked across the room to the closet. I grabbed what appeared to be the cleanest t-shirt and jeans I could find and sniffed them. Honestly, I was too tired to care. They had to be better than my previous evening's attire, still covered in vamp dust and sweat. Clothes in hand, I headed for the door. I stubbed my toe, knocking over a picture frame onto the floor. I bent over to pick it up and froze.

In the picture, Ronald and Murray stood on opposite sides of me. Ronald, sporting a goatee on his round face, had his long, tanned arms draped over our shoulders and was smiling. We all were. I sighed. It was taken right outside the front of Queen's Pawn, the day we moved into Murray's apartment—the last day I saw Ronald alive. I placed the picture back on the dresser and left.

Murray's clacking at his keyboard echoed from his bedroom. Shafts of light from the open curtains cascaded across the living room, as the sun had continued its descent into night.

Almost time for work. But first, a shower. I might smell like someone who frequents the comforts of cheap liquor and truck stop hookers, which isn't too far off base, but I believed in the gospel of soap and water.

I stepped into the bathroom, and damn near slipped on the floor—someone forgot to put a towel down. The sweet aroma of lavender and cherries assaulted my nostrils. Madison. To be honest, it almost disappointed me she wasn't there. The woman had probably left for work. In a city that never sleeps, who knows what a girl like her would be up to? What I wouldn't have given to… Shaking my head, I attempted to remove thoughts of Madison from my mind and failed.

Murray didn't need to know about my inner turmoil concerning his raven-haired paramour. I closed the toilet and placed my clothes on the lid, got in the shower, and turned on the faucet.

It didn't take long as the rivulets of water ran down my skin to realize I had bruises from the events of the previous night. The one I received from being thrown into a key stop had started to knot. Reaching for my shampoo, I found the bottle empty. At least Madison left some of hers here. *Beggars can't be choosers*. I borrowed some and ran it through my hair. I came out of the shower smelling like a cherry bath bomb that exploded at a party thrown by David Bowie. *Dance magic, dance, baby*. I'm pretty sure when I looked in the mirror glitter found its way into my hair.

Whatever.

Murray had his back to me when I stopped by the open doorway of his bedroom on the way to the kitchen. His face was glued to his computer rig with its multiple monitors as he tapped away. He didn't notice me standing there. A poster with an image of The Phoenix casino hung right above the headboard of the bed—an advertisement for *Illumination*, its orange and white lettered tagline stating, "Featuring Madison Lily".

"Finally, you're awake," Murray said, breaking me out of my trance.

"Up yours," I began, "I woke up on time."

"Yeah, I heard the alarm clock crash against the wall promptly at 7:05 p.m." Murray shook his head. "That makes six you've broken this year. This is why we can't have nice things."

"Speak for yourself, Reginald," I said, motioning with a head nod inside his room.

"Fuck you," he said.

"Thanks, but you're not my type," I quipped, ducking out of the room before Murray managed to hit me with whatever object he sent sailing through the air at my face. I chuckled and walked the short distance into the kitchen to see what I could scrounge up to eat.

My choices for provisions were not incredibly varied. The milk in the refrigerator had gone sour, we were out of beer, and whatever Murray had stored in a Tupperware container near the back I'm pretty sure contained alien life. I sighed when I found a half-eaten slice of dry toast with Madison's signature bright pink lipstick on it and groaned. At least there was coffee. I rinsed out the pot, put new grounds in the filter, turned the machine on, and waited.

"I managed to take care of that issue with the police for you," Murray said as he entered the kitchen.

Good ol' Murray. Taking care of my legal issues that arise from monster hunting. What a sweetheart.

"Thanks. But the mission failed. The target ended up dead."

Murray came over and stood next to me by the coffee maker. "Yeah, but the money deposited into our account," he said.

"Maybe we can order out, then. Like one of those giant-ass three-foot pizzas I keep seeing advertisements for," I replied. My stomach grumbled.

"Don't you think it's odd?" Murray asked.

"Not really. We got paid, it's all that matters." I glared at the coffee maker. Why does it take so long for the pot to fill? I could walk the length of the Strip and back in the time it takes this shit to percolate.

"It was a trap. Why send us after Dr. Griffin's son, only to have the mission wind up in failure?"

I frowned. "Look, maybe we received some bad intel—"

"No shit, ya think?" Murray crossed his arms as he leaned against the counter.

I smiled. It was almost adorable how he tried to look so tough and mean with his unkempt hair while wearing yesterday's pajamas.

Finally, the coffee maker finished its brewing. I grabbed a pair of plain ceramic mugs from the cabinet and poured coffee into each one. I grimaced as I sipped mine and handed the other mug to Murray. I don't see how he drinks this stuff black.

"Fine, I'll go to Norman's while I'm patrolling tonight and see what I can find out. Okay?" I set my mug on the counter before perusing the cabinets for some sugar.

Unfortunately, we were out. *Damn it all to hell.*

"Thanks. You're such a dear." Murray shook his head, and drank from his mug.

I raised an eyebrow. *Sarcasm?*

"You're welcome, Reg——"

Without looking up from his cup, Murray punched me in the arm, and I busted out laughing. I checked the time on the wall clock. 8:00 p.m. Time for work.

But first, a visit to Norman's.

An Uber dropped me off at a one-story brick building near McCarren Airport. It was a good thing our client paid us, or I would've had to walk forty-five minutes to get to Norman's. One side of the building had commissioned graffiti art depicting the darker side of Vegas nightlife. The smell of cheap beer accompanied a group of sweaty dudes looking to get laid by the bachelorette party who stumbled inside. Why the party of girls came here instead of a strip club is anyone's guess. Part of me wanted to drink whatever had convinced them coming here was a good idea.

I walked toward the entrance and caught the gaze of the 350-pound bouncer dressed in motorcycle leathers guarding the door. Lars appeared to be made of more fat than muscle, but I can assure you, from personal experience, he's definitely more Colossus than The Blob. I have the medical records from when he broke my arm to prove it. He stood under the neon-pink sign that read "Norman's" in 1950's cursive, and gave me a fist bump. Our relationship has improved over the years, mainly because we declared a cease-fire on speaking to each other.

Just like every other crowded bar of similar repute, the interior of Norman's was dimly lit, save for the bar on one side and the low-rising platform stage along the back wall. The bachelorette party sat at a table on the opposite side from the bar, full of smiles and drunken giggles. The leader of the Sweaty Dudes talked to the brunette sitting at the table with them—her tiara and sash indicating her bride-to-be status—and extended a hand to her, which she graciously accepted with a giggle-snort. I watched as the pair left out a side entrance and shook my head. Someone's marriage is about to end before it starts. Oh well, what happens in Vegas...

I admired the backside view of a scantily clad female server carrying a tray. She sauntered past, then quickly made her way over to the bar. Tally—who went by Tal—was working tonight. Her blue-dyed hair hung right below her ears, and she wore a plain black tank top and jean shorts. The woman stood maybe five-foot-nothing, wearing pleather ass-kicker boots making her at least six inches taller. With the boots and a night's worth of tips in her pockets, Tal couldn't have been more than one-hundred pounds soaking wet. The cuteness of her appearance was a deception, though. I've seen her get into an argument before with Lars. If such a disagreement between the behemoth outside and the pint-sized pixie of a woman behind the bar ever came to blows, my money would be on Tal.

"What'll it be, Apollo? The usual?"

"No thanks, Tal, I don't have time to drink the cheap swill you serve here."

"It's never bothered you before."

She had me there. I had built up quite a tab on cheap beer while waiting on job opportunities from clients.

"What's up with your—" I pointed at the elf ears affixed to the sides of her head. Combined with the blue hair, Tal looked like the epitome of the girls from one of those anime shows Murray was so keen on watching.

"Oh these, I attended a fantasy convention at one of the hotels on the Strip earlier today," she said.

I raised an eyebrow. "I didn't know you were into that kind of thing,"

"I'm not, but my boyfriend is." The grin on her face curled into a smirk. She leaned forward on the bar, attempting to squeeze together those acorns she called breasts into something resembling cleavage.

"You have a boyfriend?"

Tal always seemed to be the type to play for an all-girls team. Not like it mattered.

"I did for the past eight hours," Tal snickered. "I'm past it though. Stuck with the ears for now. Spirit gum is incredibly difficult to take off without the right kind of remover."

I grinned. "Some people here might find the ears hot, maybe you'll get more tips."

"Are you sure you're in the right kind of club, Sparkles?" she asked. Looking at my reflection in the mirror, I scowled. There *was* glitter in my hair. Dammit, Madison.

"Is Norman here?"

"Yeah, he's in the back. Should I…" Tal nodded toward the hallway behind the bar.

I tapped the bar and took a step back. "No need. I know the way."

The hallway behind the bar was as seedy as one would expect in this kind of establishment. The posters and stickers advertising shows and events adorning the walls were long since outdated. On one side of the hallway a set of swinging doors led into the kitchen, and I heard laughter from the staff. I grimaced as I walked past the bathrooms on the other side. At least I took a shower and did my business before I came here. Then again, anyone who used the toilets here and lived to tell the tale were probably immune from most communicable diseases. Not wanting to test the theory, I made my way to the nondescript wooden door at the end of the hallway and entered Norman's office.

"You know, Apollo…knocking is considered appropriate manners," Norman said as I entered. He was a skinny man, his skin tanned from a lifetime of living in the desert, his receding hair-line starting to turn grey, and from the way the baggy tie-dyed T-shirt he wore above his jeans hung on his frame, he could stand to eat a cheeseburger.

"Since when have you known me to be appropriate?" I asked, looking about the room. Think about every private investigator's office in every detective noir film you've seen. Cover the windows in blackout curtains, add a bowl of burning sage sitting in the middle of the desk to ward off magics of evil denizens, and you have Norman's office down to a T.

"Fair enough," he replied. "What do you want? I told you I'd call you when a job came up. You should've already been paid for last night."

I shook my head as I moved to stand in front of the desk. "You mean the botched mission that got Connor Griffin killed?" It wasn't like Norman to send us on a fool's errand. Murray and I had been working for him ever since Ronald died, and something about the way last night's events unfolded struck me as strange.

Norman shrugged. "You got your money, so what's the deal?"

"Funny, Murray said the same thing to me earlier

this evening," I said, "The point is, why did the client give us bad intel?"

Another shrug from Norman. "Does it matter? You got your money," he said. Something about the worried tone I picked up on in Norman's voice bothered me.

"Norman—"

Norman looked straight at me and shook his head. "Please go. You don't want to get involved."

"What's going on?" I asked, equal parts confused and infuriated. I slammed my hands on the desk. "Damnit, Norman! "I'm not leaving until I get some answers!" My voice echoed off the walls. Norman's eyes went wide, but he remained silent.

Time for a more direct approach.

"Why was I set up?" I slammed the desk again. This time, the bowl of sage tipped over.

There, I said it. Screw microphones. I dropped the fucking gauntlet.

If Norman wasn't the only sober person in the bar besides myself, he would've peed his pants from witnessing the blind rage on my face. Hell, he might have already. I couldn't tell. Those jeans were kind of dark. Not that I cared. "They already have the doctor!" he shouted, stumbling back and landing in the cracked faux-leather cushioned chair sitting behind him. "The kid was going to die anyway as punishment!"

"Who's 'they'?" It took quite an effort not to growl.

"I can't say," Norman said.

"Norman!" I didn't have time for games.

"I swear, Apollo, I can't." Norman's eyes grew wide, and if he shifted any further back in the chair, he was going to end up going through the damn thing. "But you need to get ready. A storm is brewing," he said warily.

"Stop fucking with me and spouting off your cryptic bullshit," I spat.

Norman's gaze shifted from me to the sage bowl that tipped over, and I started to understand. Not fully, but started to. Someone with magic more powerful than the defense the sage provided came in, performed an enchantment, a glamour most likely, and was preventing Norman from telling me the full truth. Damn it all to hell.

The vampires from the Coven had set me up, and I wanted to know why. Storming out of the office, I growled with frustration. Tal waved at me as I rushed past the bar, but I didn't acknowledge her. Murray and I had been looking for Dr. Griffin for the past year, and the vampires already had him. Once in the parking lot, I strode several places away from the bar, and called Murray.

His angered voice when I relayed my conversation with Norman made it clear he was as pissed off as me.

3

"You've got to be shitting me," Murray said as I got in his car. It was a cherry-red beat-up piece of shit '96 Ford Fiesta that I had to slide the seat all the way back so I could climb in and sit down. Here I am, six feet tall, and trying to fit into a vehicle the size of a roller-skate. At least if it ran out of gas, I'd be able to pick it up and carry it.

"Trust me, I'm not," I replied. The seatbelt wouldn't budge and I didn't feel like screwing with it. I leaned back in the passenger seat as he drove us away from Norman's and seriously reconsidered saving money to get my car out of the shop. If I had the money to save, that is.

"I wonder who the hell is fucking with us," he said.

"Hell if I know. It's the million-dollar question right now," I replied. We approached a stoplight, and the strained expression on Murray's face told me he wanted to disregard the signal entirely.

"Then they can pay us a million dollars." Murray's voice remained tense. I understood his frustration. I could have walked back to the Strip from Norman's faster. Murray reached into the back seat and damn near hit me with the leather jacket he shoved in my direction. "Here, take this."

"Aww, Snookums, you shouldn't have," I said in the sweetest voice possible, which for a man with a low tenor voice like me, didn't come easily. I examined the jacket's interior pockets. Murray had kindly loaded it with a few extra stakes and some thin chains of silver. How kind. I put the jacket on, pretending it was my battle armor. Essentially, it was. While I knew I looked good in the leather pants, I praised myself for remembering to put on jeans tonight. I had no desire to come home smelling like rancid sewer ass two nights in a row.

Murray rolled his eyes. "Whatever, just make sure this lasts longer than one night. These jackets are expensive as hell to clean and I'm running out of excuses to borrow money from my parents."

"You're such a doll, Reginald," I said, casting a half-smile glance in his direction.

"Asshole," he replied as the light finally turned green.

I held a hand to my heart, shaking my head as I whispered softly, "A truer word has never been spoken."

Murray burst out laughing at my response as we headed toward the Strip. This is how our friendship had always been, back and forth banter only the best of friends could maintain. Except now, I had to be somewhat cautious. Ronald wasn't around anymore to act as a buffer when I accidentally—correction, purposefully—crossed the line. I mean, egging Murray on is one of my favorite pastimes.

Ten years ago, Ronald and I arrived in Vegas for the first time. We rolled into town on a whim and a prayer. However, we used the last of our money on a not-so-cheap hooker, and as a result were unable to afford tickets to fly home. That's when we met Murray. We found him at a blackjack table in the casino level of Circus Circus one night, and joined the game to be dealt in. I'm a shit player, but Ronald was fantastic. I wouldn't say publicly he was good enough to count cards, but...

Then again, the same could be said for Murray.

This might have caused an incident back then in which security came to our table. I might have punched a security guard, and Ronald and I might have landed in jail as a result while Murray ran away. Possibly. That might have happened. Luckily for us, Murray expressed thanks for his escape by bailing us out, using his computer-wizard magic to make our records from getting arrested disappear. Remember when I mentioned Murray took care of my legal issues? The day I landed in jail was the first time, and he, Ronald, and I had been an inseparable trio ever since— until the day Ronald died, of course.

"I said, did you want to come with me?" Murray asked. Apparently, he had been talking the entire time I did my memory deep-dive.

"Sorry what?" I asked, blinking my eyes.

Murray rolled his eyes. "I swear, Apollo, sometimes you have shit for brains."

I snorted, and in the best imitation of a caveman voice, I said, "Me no think hard when fight bad guys." Especially vampires. Like I had told Connor the previous night, pointy end goes in the bad guy.

"Wow, you went there," Murray said.

"Did you expect anything else?"

Murray shook his head and continued driving. "Anyway, I need to head back to the shop to help the 'rents close up. You wanna call it a night?"

I shook my head. "Nah, I want to do some patrolling."

"But we don't have a client," Murray said. Good ol' Murray, always thinking about money.

"I need to blow off some steam. Drop me off here," I said as we pulled in front of the Paris. The Vegas street crowd teemed with all walks of life, from the super-rich, to people in costumes, showgirls in pasties, and yes, cowboys in assless chaps. The last one struck me as odd. I expected to see such things on say, Fremont Street, but not here in front of the Paris. This happened to be one of the classier casinos in my opinion.

Murray nodded. "Sure thing, and hey, Apollo?" he asked as I got out of the car.

"Yeah?" Running a hand through my hair, I turned around and leaned inside the passenger window. An impatient ride-share car parked behind us honked his horn, and Murray's quick reply consisted of a middle-finger salute in the rearview mirror.

"You look like a damn *Twilight* wannabe. Get any glitter on the jacket, and you're paying the next bill," Murray said. Of course, he waited until I'm running my hand through my hair to say it. Of course. Dammit, Madison.

I wondered how many more times I would curse the woman's name over my hair as Murray drove away. I shrugged and stuck my hands in the pockets of my jacket, and casually strode south along the crowded sidewalk away from the Paris toward the Bellagio. Perhaps the outdoor fountain would be on by the time I got there. Lit up by multicolored lights at night, it would definitely be a soothing sight.

I never made it to the Bellagio, not even close. I had barely made it past the Paris when three men ran past chasing someone dressed like James Dean. Either that, or the person they were running after had a strong taste for 1950's fashion. What drew me to follow had nothing to do with a possible mugging, but the three men were quickly running into a trap. After vampire hunting for a while, you learn how one moves. The guy dressed like James Dean definitely ran with more fluidity than normal for a human.

"Over here!" one of the men, who was skinnier than Norman—if such a thing were possible—and had oily hair, shouted.

"I'm coming!" shouted the short man who followed Oily-Hair. And I do mean short. Tal was taller than this guy.

"Wait for me!" The third man, a bit on the roly-poly side, exclaimed. "That pale-faced freak's ass is mine!" If there were any doubts, Roly-poly confirmed it. These three idiots were chasing a vampire. I kept a safe distance behind, but once James Dean glided swiftly behind a large dumpster, I decided to go play hero.

"What's going on back here?" I winced as soon as I asked the question. Why couldn't I have thought of something better?

"Stay out of it, man. This doesn't concern you," Oily-Hair said. His companions all turned to me, and it was apparent these fresh-faced kids were barely out of high school and not prepared to deal with the vampire who strode out from behind the dumpster.

"Actually, I think it does, unless you want to pick a fight with—him," I replied, pointing at James Dean. His face had twisted into a fanged visage as he snarled at the three men. I mean, I was upset about the news concerning Dr. Griffin, and it wasn't like I'd be getting paid. If these young punk ass-hats wanted to poke the ire of a pissed off vampire, then more power to them. Too bad I didn't bring any popcorn.

The three men turned around and saw Vamp-Dean for the first time. They screamed like little girls and went running back the way they came. As they ran past me, an odor wafted by my nose and told me one of them had peed their pants. I pulled a stake out and sighed. Mostly because I didn't want to get dust on this nice, clean jacket.

Vamp-Dean's face went back to normal. Man, if dudes were my thing, I would've hit on this guy. Other than the pale skin, with his slicked back hair, lean frame covered by a white t-shirt, blue jeans, and a brown leather jacket, he looked like he stepped off a throwback issue of *GQ*.

Back to your senses, Apollo. I raised the stake in front of me.

"Wait!" Vamp-Dean shouted, slightly catching me off guard. Since when did vampires plead? Something reeked of a trap. "I've been looking for you!"

"You found me," I grunted, holding the stake up. The vampire could rush at any time, and I needed to be ready.

"I had to get your attention somehow," the vampire said.

I raised an eyebrow. Was that nervousness I heard in his voice?

"By getting a group of ignorant assholes to chase you into an alley? Dick move." Not really. I've done worse to trap a vampire, but that's a story for another time.

Vamp-Dean shook his head. "I know where Dr. Griffin is."

"Too late, that surprise has already been ruined for me," I said.

"Look, I can't tell you where exactly the doctor is," Vamp-Dean paused and leaned against the dumpster, crossing his arms. "Lower the damn stake. If I was going to attack you, Apollo, I would have done it by now."

"Didn't realize we were on a first name basis—"

"Wayne," Vamp-Dean said. A vampire named Wayne? Hilarious.

"Whatever," I said, cautiously lowering the stake. I kept it in a tight grip at my side—you know, just in case.

"All I'm permitted to tell you is the person who has him under control has already put him to work," Wayne said, shifting his eyes around nervously. What could concern a vampire more than a hunter standing in front of him with a stake?

"How do you know this?" I asked. "And why should I trust you?" They were both valid questions, and I began to feel like I was going in circles with Wayne.

"I can't really answer…but look!" Wayne pulled the sleeve of his jacket up as he extended his arm. I immediately recognized the three thin claw marks—a mark of an elder vampire—evenly spaced on his wrist. Damn. An elder vampire had glamoured Wayne into leading me here. Probably the same one who had played me by using Norman.

"Shit," I said, examining Wayne's wrist from where I stood. What I saw pissed me off. Those claw marks. The last time I had seen them…It hit me as I looked around the alley. Why hadn't I recognized it before? The dumpster, the lighting, the graffiti.

I walk the streets of Las Vegas nightly, yet always manage to find a way to avoid this alley.

This was the place where Ronald died.

Something told me whoever was trying to send me a

message didn't happen to be my newly acquired vampire pal.

"Are you going to kill me?" Wayne asked.

I shook my head and put the stake away. "No, it's not worth it," I said. "Get out of here before I change my mind. And Wayne, if you need to find me again, don't do something dumb like that shit you pulled tonight."

Wayne nodded at me wide-eyed and ran off. I grimaced and started the long walk back toward the Queen's Pawn. No need to call Murray on this one. I needed the time to figure out the best way to explain those claw marks.

4

It was nearly one in the morning by the time I made it back to the Queen's Pawn. The shop had closed hours ago. Lights inside the store windows were dimmed and the lock gate had already been pulled down over the front door. The parking lot stood eerily quiet, which didn't bother me in the slightest. The news about Dr. Griffin had upset me, never mind the fact whoever was screwing with me might be responsible for Ronald's death. Too upset to be pissed, I just wanted to go to sleep.

Murray pulled into the small lot behind the shop as I placed my hand on the metal banister to the stairs leading up to our apartment.

"Where the hell have you been? Shouldn't you already be here?" I asked as Murray got out of the car. He had plastic grocery bags in each hand.

"Shut it. I went to get more groceries after helping close the shop," Murray said. "Here." He shoved the lighter of the two bags forcefully at me.

"What's this?" Looking in the bag, I found a nondescript bottle containing something…green. The only light nearby was the emergency lights on the back of the shop, and they weren't exactly the greatest source of illumination.

"I got us more shampoo," Murray replied. "I can't keep having you coming out of the bathroom smelling like my girlfriend."

Snickering, I made kissy faces at Murray. "Oh, come on, you like the glitter look on me," I said.

Murray sighed. "You're getting glitter shit all over the jacket."

I shrugged my shoulders. "Hey, at least it's not vampire dust, or worse…blood."

Murray leaned his head back and groaned as he started up the stairs.

"How was your night?"

"Oh, you know, casual walk on the Strip, flirted with a few ladies, discovered an elder vampire is in town—"

"What?!" My roommate paused halfway up the steps, turning to look at me. Tried anyway. He stood several steps up. If I didn't pause in time, I would have had me a face full of Murray. We both nervously coughed. "How do you know this?" he asked.

"Some James Dean lookalike vamp chased me down. He had claw marks on his wrist, exactly like the ones—"

"Shit" He turned around and headed back up the stairs. We both remained silent as we approached the door of the apartment. Neither of us wanted to remember that night ten years ago. It was the night we encountered a gang of vampires bearing the same mark. Vampires who killed Ronald. Murray stopped going on hunts soon after, leaving me to deal with all the physical work while he did all the technical stuff.

"What's this?" Murray picked up a plain white envelope sticking out from the bottom of the door.

"I don't know. Let me see," I said.

Murray handed me the envelope, and I popped off the wax seal and pulled out the folded card tucked inside. We entered the apartment, and I sat on the couch while Murray put the rest of the groceries away. Opening the card, I took a moment to read its contents. The handwriting on the page was a beautiful, flowing script of damn-near perfect penmanship.

Mr. Apollo Grant,

You are cordially invited to attend our celebration at the Phoenix tomorrow on Thursday, nine o' clock in the evening, as our Guest of Honor. I wish to applaud you for your efforts in keeping this city secure and do hope you will attend. Show this invitation at the door and ask for room 1501 at the front desk.

I look forward to meeting you.

Please feel free to bring a guest.

The invitation didn't end in a signature. What should I make of it? Thursday was tomorrow—well technically today since it was well past the witching hour. The complete and utter bullshit of this nonsense was too coincidental. *Okay elder vampire, whoever you are, what do you want from me?*

"What's it say?" Murray walked into the living room.

I handed the card to him. His brow furrowed as he read the invitation, then handed it back to me.

"This is most definitely a trap, Apollo. I'd be careful. I can only do so much for you if things go south, but I can't do anything for you if you're dead."

I nodded in agreement. Murray wasn't exactly wrong. However, the more I thought about it, the more I knew the invitation would be my best shot at finding some answers.

"It's worth the risk. I'm going anyway. Wanna be my date?" I grinned at Murray.

"No thanks. I think I'll pass. I look smashing in a suit, and I'd make you look bad," Murray quipped.

"Guess I'll go alone, then," I muttered, leaning my head back in mock destitution.

"Do me a favor though," Murray said.

I raised an eyebrow. "What's that?"

"If you happen to catch Madison between shows, can you make sure she's alright? She hasn't texted me back today."

"Yeah, if I see her."

Murray sneered mockingly at me before leaving the room. I giggled when I heard the door to his room slam shut. Smiling, I nestled back into the couch. No point in going to bed early. Might as well stay up for a few hours and enjoy the sunrise before I went to bed. I had plenty of time until the party.

I didn't get to see the sunrise. Passing out on the couch, I was soon greeted by dreams of Ronald, Madison, and the indistinguishable visage of the mystery elder vampire who wanted nothing more than to screw with my head.

———

I arrived thirty minutes early to the Phoenix. I should have bummed whatever money we had left from our last job for an Uber. But no, Murray had turned in early for the night by the time I woke up, and I walked the entire way in a dark suit jacket and pants, and yes—dress shoes. It was hot, I sweated profusely, and my ass didn't look nearly as awesome as it does in leather. I mean, it looked good. At least I didn't have glitter in my hair.

The Phoenix was a modest hotel and casino combination when compared to the much larger establishments located on the Strip. It had maybe a quarter of the number of hotel floors when compared to say, the Paris. The throngs of people outside the casino entrance when I arrived made it hard to tell. This was one of the trendiest spots in town, and people dressed in their best glam were lined up around the hotel behind a velvet rope. Straightening my jacket, I felt the front to make sure the stakes I had brought as insurance were there and walked up to the entrance.

A bouncer standing by the rope blockade who could have been one of Lars's brothers placed a hand on my chest, preventing me from going inside.

"Sorry pal, show's not open yet. Go wait in line." The bouncer pushed me back a few steps.

"Oh, yeah. Here." I took the invitation out of the interior pocket of my jacket and showed it to the bouncer.

"Oh! Mr. Grant, please proceed," the bouncer said, handing the invitation back to me.

He bowed. I walked past, tucking the invitation back into my suit jacket. I'll admit, I grimaced a little at the way he addressed me. My name is Apollo. Mr. Grant was my father. And the two of us hadn't spoken since I left home over a decade ago. Pushing thoughts of my strained relationship with my father aside, I entered the casino-level entrance of the Phoenix.

I've been to about every casino there is in Las Vegas, save for the Phoenix. But this place was something different altogether. Multicolored lights hung overhead, and some musical fusion of rock and modern-pop played through the speakers. Evenly spaced amongst the various types of slot machines and games were small tables with poles in the center that reached to the ceiling. And on every one of those tables a female dancer twirled lithely around a pole. I've been to my fair share of gentlemen's clubs, but the way these ladies worked those poles could've given the most high-class stripper a run for their money.

The lack of smoke also struck me as odd. I don't think I've ever been in a Vegas casino that didn't reek of stale cigarettes embedded into the carpet. I had to pinch myself to make sure this wasn't a dream. Now my cheek hurt. Yeah, I was definitely not dreaming. I enjoyed the view of one particular dancer wearing a pink, pig-tailed wig and thigh-high white platforms for a moment—and I'm pretty sure she winked at me. Then remembered my purpose here had nothing to do with her delightful and flirtatious come-hither dance. Maybe she would be here when my business was over.

I walked over to the front desk, where a spindly little man in standard hotel business attire—black jacket, white shirt, and black pants—was standing. He looked up at me and pushed his glasses up his nose.

"Can I help you, sir?" the attendant asked. He reminded me of my old English teacher from high school. The way he whined made it sound like there was glass scratching at the back of his throat.

"Yes, I was told to ask for room 1501," I said.

The man lowered his eyes. "Sir, this hotel only has thirteen floors."

Sighing, I took the invitation back out of my jacket and showed it to the man. I didn't have any more time for bullshit games. "Look, it says right here on the card—"

"The floors stop at thirteen," he said, turning his back to me to get something from one of the drawers.

"But—"

I stopped when the man turned around, took the invitation from me, and pressed a rectangular plastic keycard into my hand.

"Your keycard sir, down the hall and to the right." He motioned with an arm toward a hallway off to the side. "You'll find the elevator, as requested."

The man resumed whatever he was doing before I walked over, essentially ignoring me while I stood there dumbfounded. I headed toward the hallway, reminding myself not to sneak any last-minute looks at the dancers on the tables behind me. I was walking into a trap, and I couldn't afford any more distractions. Following the attendant's directions to the elevators, I pressed the up arrow, and waited as the display over the door showed one of the lifts moving up from two levels below the ground floor. I was pleasantly surprised I managed to make here this far without incident.

The doors opened.

Madison stood there, in all of her raven-haired voluptuous glory. We locked stares with each other, and I no longer had to imagine what she looked like in a show-girl outfit. Or what little of the beaded fabric she wore attempted to call itself an outfit, anyway. I think the silver heeled stilettos she wore provided more coverage. Someone remind me again how Murray landed the hot chick? Please.

"Apollo," she said as I stepped inside.

"Madison," I turned around—both to press the button to close the elevator door, and to hide the fact that 'little Apollo' currently was standing front and center. "Fancy seeing you here." I managed to spit out. Damn, this woman made me nervous.

"Likewise." She reached in front of me to press the button before I got a chance.

I searched for the button for my floor. No floor fifteen. I glanced at the card in my hand, and saw the card said 1501 on it, but underneath it in small print said *thirteenth floor.* Who the hell designed this hotel? Shrugging, I pressed the button for the thirteenth floor and we made our ascent.

"Shouldn't you be in a show tonight?" I asked.

"It got cancelled." Madison voice cooed. "The sound system isn't working, so I was going to a friend's hotel room to change before heading back to Murray's."

I dared to take a step back, turning my head to look at her. "There's one hell of a line of people outside who are going to be super pissed about that."

Madison shook her head and shrugged. "Not my issue, I'm simply a dancer in the show. My manager can take care of those ramifications. Anyway, what are you doing here?" she asked as she turned to face me.

"I got invited to a party," I said bluntly.

"Apollo Grant, you don't do parties," she replied, and I opened the side of my jacket, revealing the stakes I had hidden there. "Oh," she whispered.

Madison stumbled toward me as movement suddenly ground to a halt, pressing me against the side wall. The lights went out.

"Shit," was all I managed to say.

5

"Apollo, I don't think what's jabbing the inside of my thigh are those stakes in your jacket," Madison said.

I put the keycard into my back pocket and pulled out my cellphone, turning on the flashlight to provide some sort of illumination. The woman had me awkwardly pressed against the wall of the elevator, and as I came to the conclusion that the fullness of her breasts pressing through my dress shirt were one hundred percent real, part of me wished I had pulled out something other than my cellphone. Madison coughed nervously and took a few steps back. I set my phone face down on the ground. It cast its eerie white light from the flash across the small area.

Madison pressed the panic button on the control panel. Nothing happened.

"This is like that one time I was in New Orleans," she sighed.

I stood up straight from where I was leaning and

smoothed out more than my jacket. "You were stuck in a tight space with a devilishly handsome man?"

Madison rolled her eyes and scoffed, "Don't flatter yourself. It's unbecoming."

Rude.

"Those doors aren't going to open until the power comes back on," I said.

"Whatever, I don't see you doing anything," Madison replied.

Oh, I was doing something all right. Crossing my arms, I took in a moment to delight myself with the beauty of the curves belonging to the woman standing in front of me. The way the light from my cellphone cast its brilliance off of her dress—what little of it hung on her; it was practically nothing more than nipple pasties and strung beads—made her look like a goddess. Especially with the glitter in her hair. Hair that cascaded in waves down to the small of her back, drawing my attention to a quite pleasing posterior. My pants began tightening again, and I gulped. *Damn, Murray, I'm fucking jealous of you if this is what comes home to you most nights.*

As Madison continued to desperately fiddle with the door, I remained where I was, reflecting on the first time I had met the woman. It was about a month after Ronald had died, and we were already working for Norman. That's a story for another day, but Norman basically witnessed the whole thing with Ronald go down and brought us in as hunters-for-hire. He had sent us on a mission to take care of some vamps causing trouble with some of the tourists on Fremont Street. Murray and I were enjoying dinner from one of the restaurants in the area when I witnessed Madison being followed into a dark alley by the vamps in question and decided to go save the day.

When I got to the corner, Madison had fallen to the ground, and was waving one of her six-inch stilettos wildly in the air in an attempt to fend off her attackers. I took care of the vampires quickly, but after I turned them to dust and she opened her eyes, Murray had finally caught up. He was the one she saw first, and well…that's how all my bad luck with Madison Lily started.

"Damn door won't open!" Madison exclaimed as she alternated between pulling on the doors and pressing the panic button.

"You know," I said, scratching my head, "we could be patient and wait for the power to come back on."

"Thanks, Captain Fucking Obvious," Madison sneered. "Now, stop being an ass and come help me with this."

"Such language is not very ladylike."

Madison twirled around, beads flaring out on their strings as she spun, and stopped to stare straight at me in such a way I knew my attempt at sounding innocent had failed. No matter, the view of her front side was just as enjoyable.

I shrugged, standing up straight. "Fine, but I'm telling you, we're stuck here for now."

Madison rolled her eyes. "Just shut up and help." She slinked her way over to the side as I stepped over to the door. We each took a door and pulled. No dice. Madison spewed a string of profanities that would have made a sailor blush, but I was paying more attention to the way she bounced in those heels as she verbally assaulted the elevator. I shook my head. Even pissed off, her words sounded like honey.

"Done with your little tantrum there?" I asked.

"Whatever, let's try this again," Madison said.

I shrugged. *Okay, Sugar-tits, but these doors are stuck until the power comes back on.*

Then I was proven wrong. The elevator doors opened on their own, aided by the help of a surprising, but familiar face.

"Wayne?" I asked. He still had that James Dean look about him, even though today he wore more formal attire—a gray suit with the jacket hanging open to reveal a black shirt. Was I going to question my own sexuality every time I encountered this dude? A quick glance over to Madison assured me otherwise.

"Figured I'd eventually find you here," he said, squatting from his perch on the edge of the ninth floor. The floor was positioned about halfway up the door opening.

Tilting my head, I said, "I don't know if I should be appreciative, or worried you're following me."

Wayne smiled. "Let's just say I have a vested interest in your safety." He extended an arm toward Madison "Ma'am," he said, pulling her up. Coincidentally, it was in such a way I found myself not entirely displeased to receive a face full of her behind as she was lifted. I had to take a step back though, since I wasn't too keen on finding out if those heels were capable of stabbing my eye—or anything else important.

"Don't call me that, old man," she said once she finished making it out.

"Just because I'm older than your parents don't make me an old man," Wayne replied.

I picked up my cellphone. "You know him?" I asked Madison after Wayne pulled me out of the shaft into the hallway. It was like those creepy hallways in horror movies when all of a sudden, everything, including the emergency lights, went out.

"Yeah, he's been a regular since the Phoenix

opened," Madison replied. I stared at her cautiously. *Yes, because it's totally normal to be on friendly terms with a vampire. Nothing strange about it at all.*

"Madison, he's—"

"A vampire? I know. Who cares? Not like I haven't been around them before, especially with what you and Murray do for a living."

I had to admit, she got me there. She'd seen me come home a time or two covered in more than vamp dust.

Wayne brushed some dust off of his jacket. "Look Apollo, you're going into a trap." He looked at me, then to Madison, who rolled her eyes, then back to me.

"Again, a bit late to the party." I eyed Wayne up and down. "Besides, how do I know you didn't leave the invitation on my doorstep?"

"Trust me, I'm not the one who delivered it," Wayne said, holding his hands up in mock defense. The sleeve of his jacket slid down, exposing the claw marks on his wrist again. This time, they seemed to be glowing.

I shook my head. A vampire asking me, a hunter-for-hire to trust him? I probably would have staked him right there if he hadn't been standing so close to Madison. Then again, those heels did appear to be pointy enough, and probably were made of wood. Also, I liked this suit.

"Apollo, he's telling the truth, he's been here at the Phoenix all night," she said. "Wayne is our lead sound technician for *Illumination.*"

As if on cue, Wayne bowed with a flourish.

Right, the show she's headlining. Well, isn't that convenient. "Funny a vampire is working at a place named after a fire bird and is part of a show of which the name literally means 'to light'," I said. Then again, my parents named me after a sun god and I hunt vampires and other creatures. Hilarious.

There was a buzzing sound, and we all gave a start as the lights came back on.

No sooner did that happen before the power went back out. *Great, just perfect, because it's not like whoever invited me here isn't already toying with me.* At least this time, the emergency lights stayed on.

"Now what?" Madison asked.

I shrugged. "I have a party to get to. Something tells me shit's going to go down if I'm any later than I already am."

"Knowing you, Apollo, it's already going down," Madison said, snickering as she held a hand up to her mouth.

"Want me to come along with you?" Wayne asked.

"I didn't ask for your help," I replied.

Wayne scoffed, "You'd be stuck in the elevator if I hadn't shown up."

"Maybe someone doesn't want you to go, Apollo," Madison said.

I shook my head. "Unlikely. This is someone who knows where I live, knows what I do. Fucked up my last job on purpose. Sent this James Dean lookalike here to follow me twice now. I need to find another way up."

Wayne raised both his eyebrows, admiring himself in a hallway mirror while slicking his hair back. Yes, contrary to popular belief, vampires can see their own reflection. "Hey, I look good," he said.

"That wasn't a compliment," I said.

"Emergency stairs are at the end of the hall," Madison motioned with her arm toward the end of the hallway.

I immediately started heading in the direction she

indicated to find the stairs. No way in hell I'd be getting on the elevator again, even if the power did come back on. Given recent events, the temptation to listen to my manhood instead of my brain held too much risk.

They both stared at me when I opened the door to the stairwell. Wayne especially so in a somewhat peculiar fashion. I sighed. I had four flights of stairs to climb and something told me I was going to need back-up for whatever I was about to encounter.

"Are you coming or not?" I asked, and almost regretted doing so. The invitation did say to bring a guest. And from my personal experience, vampires weren't exactly weak.

Wayne entered the stairwell, and Madison took a step forward.

"I wasn't talking to you, Madison."

Madison glared at me and placed her hands on her hips. "Please. I dance every night in these heels with fifty-pound angel wings on my back. I think I can manage some stairs." Well, damn. Something about the way Madison spoke made me stare at her eyes and not the near-nakedness of her costume. She wasn't going to take no for an answer, and I felt too blue-balled to argue.

"Excuse me," Wayne said sheepishly before ascending the stairs.

"I'm not stupid," Madison said, taking off her heels before sauntering past me to follow Wayne. "Someone has to keep an eye on you, and I don't want you accidentally killing my sound guy."

And here I was beginning to think you didn't have an issue with me hunting creatures of the night. Another perfectly positioned view of Madison's ass blessed me as she climbed the stairs, and I ran past her to catch up to Wayne before my manhood got any ideas.

Right before we reached the access door to floor twelve, I slowed down to allow Madison to catch up. Honestly, I had genuine concern, I swear. I wasn't trying to get a look at her—

A nice close-up view of Madison's breasts engulfed me as the entirety of the woman's cleavage hugged my face. I stood there for several moments, stunned. Not that I was complaining, but not exactly what I expected, either.

"Apollo!" Madison exclaimed.

"Sorry," I said, almost as a question as she pushed me back. I had to maintain a tight grip on the railing to keep from plummeting. Although, given my recent embarrassment, it almost seemed like the safer alternative.

"I'm going to go on ahead," Wayne shook his head, grinning, and continued up the next flight.

"Why did you stop?" Madison huffed.

"Look, I just wanted to make sure you were okay," I said.

Madison raised an eyebrow. "What, do you think I'm some kind of damsel in distress?"

"No, but—"

"Ugh," she grunted as she shook her head.

"Guys, we have an issue, this door won't open," Wayne shouted from the next flight up. Madison and I made our way quickly up the last flight of stairs and met my new vampire companion by the floor thirteen access door. He was struggling with the door, it appeared to be held in place by some kind of access card mechanism.

"Can't you use your super vamp strength to pry it open?" I asked.

Wayne scowled at me. "I'm a vampire, not Hercules.

Besides, I used all of my extra strength rescuing you kids."

"Who're you calling a kid?" Madison asked. I couldn't tell if she was being angry, or defiant. Perhaps it was a bit of both.

"Anyway, this might be the end of the road. We 're going to need an access card to get through this door," Wayne said dejectedly.

I looked at the access mechanism. It seemed simple enough, red light on the top, area to swipe a card. *That's right, I have the card I got from the front desk in my pocket.* I had no idea if this was going to work, but something had to be better than nothing.

"Here, let me try," I said, taking out the keycard from my pocket.

"Do I want to know why you have that?" Madison asked.

"Probably not," I replied, and slid the card down before anyone else had the chance to protest. After all, I had no idea who wanted me to show up here in the first place, a party I already arrived late to.

Sure enough, sliding the keycard in the door worked. The light turned green and sounded with a *click*, allowing me to turn the handle and open the door. There's a joke in here, a vampire, a showgirl, and a hunter show up to a party…

I wasn't expecting the carnage spread out on the other side when I walked onto floor thirteen, Wayne and Madison following behind. The smell nearly overcame me, and it took an extreme amount of effort not to immediately wretch.

"Oh, shit," Madison said, almost breathlessly.

'Oh, shit' was right.

Lying on the floor were a lot of dead bodies.

The thirteenth floor of the Phoenix wasn't a series of hotel rooms lined along the hallway like the floors beneath it, but rather a giant-ass party suite with a few private rooms off in the back, near an elevator entrance. A floor to ceiling glass window stood in place of the eastern wall, a small bar next to it. A few mirror balls hung from the ceiling. Tables spread about the room contained half-finished cocktails that didn't end up dropped on the floor. It seemed like a smashing party I would've loved to attend, if it weren't for the fact most of its attendees were lying dead on the floor. Damn, there was a lot of blood.

I glanced behind me, and saw Wayne standing next to Madison, his faced transformed into its uglier vampire visage. "What the hell, Wayne?"

"Apollo, there's more than dead humans here," Wayne snarled. Stepping carefully around the room, I confirmed his assessment of the dead. Traces of vampire dust lay scattered about, mixing in with the slowly spreading pools of blood. Noticing the concern on my face, he continued, "If I was going to drink her, don't you think I would have tried by now?"

"I hardly need protecting," Madison said smoothly.

Woman, have you seen yourself in a mirror lately? Hell, if I was a vampire, I would have drunk you dry by now.

I took another careful step forward and ended up slipping in congealed blood. I landed face first on the body of a brunette I might have considered extremely attractive if she had been alive. The sash across her front had been torn, and her tiara sat askew on the top of her head, but I immediately recognized her as the bride from

Norman's the other night. Someone's marriage got off to a bad start.

Madison stepped away from Wayne and remained close behind me as I continued looking around the room for any sign of what happened. I found her cherry and lavender perfume intoxicating.

"This is one hell of a party I missed," I whispered aloud.

"No shit, ya think?" Madison scoffed. I cast a sideways glance in her direction and saw her shake her head.

Wayne examined one of the corpses on the ground, then stood up, wiping blood on the side of his pants. With him being a vampire, I was surprised he didn't lick his fingers as if this was nothing more than a pile of buffalo wings. "Nothing here either," he said plainly.

"Figures." I leaned in close to Wayne. "Remind me again why you're helping?" I asked.

Wayne did one of those silent laughs only people who are purposefully hiding something can pull off. "Like I said earlier, I have a vested interest in your well-being."

Raising an eyebrow, I asked, "Care to explain?"

"You'll know soon enough," Wayne said plainly, tilting his head to the side as his face relaxed to his more human appearance.

Madison and I exchanged glances, and the woman simply shrugged at me. I furrowed my brow, scowling. I didn't have time for any more of this cryptic bullshit.

"I'm going to look around over here while you boys sort this out."

I stared at Madison as she strutted away to one of the private rooms in the back, and took pleasure in watching as she bent over to place her heels on the floor before opening the door. Casting a glance at Wayne, I found him also staring with equal intensity.

"What?" Wayne asked, raising an eyebrow.

Shrugging my shoulders, I said, "I dunno, I just—"

"I'm a vampire. I'm not blind. I'm capable of enjoying beauty when I see it," Wayne said. I couldn't help but laugh in response.

Great, I'm befriending a vampire in the middle of a bloodbath while we are both admiring the view of the behind of my room-mate's girlfriend. It could be worse, I suppose.

"Hey boys!" Madison shouted cautiously from the doorway to the private room. Wayne and I exchanged glances and walked over. What we saw surprised us both.

"This certainly is odd," Wayne said flatly.

It sure absolutely fucking is. Madison and Wayne remained standing near the outside of the doorway as I entered the room. The interior was pristine. Not a speck of blood to be found. Not. A. Single. One. White walls, white furniture, even a king-sized bed in the center with a white comforter. The hairs on the back of my neck stood upright. Someone wanted me to find this room on purpose. I waited on the door behind me to close. Surprisingly, it didn't.

"What the ever-loving fuck happened here?!" A man's voice shouted from the main room. I recognized the voice instantly. Three uniformed Las Vegas police officers entered from the stairwell door. The one who spoke stared straight into the room where I stood, looking directly at me. It was the same officer I had encountered in the Paris the night Connor died. *Well shit, party's over.*

Wayne turned to look at the officers making their way toward us. "Hang on, I'll take care of this," he said.

"Excuse me?" Madison and I both asked in unison.

"I'm a vampire, remember? I can compel them to not be any trouble." Wayne stood straight and walked over to the officers. "Gentleman…" his voice trailed off, and I tuned out his conversation with the police while I continued my search of the room. The only thing seemingly out of place was a sealed invitation envelope sitting on the center of the mattress.

"What's this?" I asked aloud.

Madison looked at me with caution "What's what?" she asked.

I showed her the envelope, and she shrugged. I popped it open, and pulled out the slip of paper tucked away inside. I don't scare easily, but I recognized the handwriting instantly, and the words on the page shook me to my core.

Sorry, I forgot the blackjack and hookers, was all the message said.

Ronald? What the hell?

6

Madison ordered an Uber for us, and we rode back to the Queen's Pawn in silence. She wore my jacket, preventing temptation for me to stare at her tits the entire ride back. It became hard to tell what made me more uncomfortable, riding in the backseat with the woman, or sitting in the middle between her and Wayne. I didn't remember asking him to come along, but I wasn't going to argue with the man who just pulled the vampire equivalent of a Jedi mind trick with the police. I mean seriously, I owe him some mad props. That's some pretty potent shit vampires can do if they're able to convince officers of the law a room full of bodies was completely normal. Then, again, we were in Vegas. I'll probably hear about it on the news tomorrow.

We made it to our destination without incident.

"I need to change clothes, and get some rest," Madison said, unlocking the apartment door and going inside. I heard her slam what I assumed was the door to Murray's bedroom. Wayne stepped around me and moved to follow.

"Whoa, what the fuck do you think you're doing?" I asked, placing my hand on Wayne's chest. He stopped and looked at me with one of those shit-eating grins only smart-asses like myself are capable of pulling off.

"Going inside," Wayne replied.

I laughed. "Not without an invitation, you're not." Seriously, that's like Vampire 101, can't cross the threshold unless—

Wayne stepped around me and entered the apartment. It took me a moment to realize what had happened before I realized my jaw was hanging open in surprise.

"Grandpa!" Murray shouted, running up to hug the vampire as I entered the apartment, closing the door behind me out of habit. *What the hell did he just say?*

"Someone want to explain to me what the hell is going on here?" I asked angrily. I needed explanations and my patience was running thin.

Murray grinned sheepishly and ran a hand through his hair. "Yeah, man, about that…"

"Reginald…" I cautioned.

Wayne and Murray both turned to look at me with a raised eyebrow. Their expressions damn near matched.

Murray sighed, "Apollo, I've been meaning to tell you about this—"

"Reginald Wayne Murray," Wayne said, extending an arm forward for a handshake. I did not accept the offer. "Remember when I told you I had a vested interest in your well-being? This man here is my grandson."

It took me a second to comprehend what the vampire in front of me said. Wayne draped his arm around Murray, and that's when I saw the resemblance. *Shit, now there are two of them.* Granted, Murray was a bit thinner than Wayne, but anyone who wasn't a dumbass would have no difficulty telling if they were related. I relaxed a little bit as I stood upright, and headed into the kitchen. I didn't know what I would find, and I would settle for coffee, anything to get the bad taste out of my mouth.

"Remember when we first met, I told you my parents named me after my grandfather? Now you know why I hate it when you call me Reginald."

"Hey!" Wayne wrinkled his face at Murray.

I glanced back at both of the Murrays. "I get it. I'd hate it if I was named after a vampire too."

"Not cool, man," Murray protested.

I shrugged. "Like I care." I closed a cabinet door and sighed. After a shitty night, I find out my roommate's grandfather is a vampire, and there's not even a damn cup of coffee in this place to distract me from it.

Murray scoffed, then joined me in the kitchen. "Be nice, Apollo. Grandpa Wayne here is half the reason why you stay out of trouble with the cops. I'm good with hacking into some things, but every once in a while, I need extra assistance."

So that's how he does it, I thought as I stared at my roommate flatly.

"I've been watching out for my family ever since the day I turned," Wayne said. He moved into the living room and laid out on the couch.

"Anyway, since now you know, don't think you can call me Reginald anymore, okay?" Murray asked.

Wayne shouted from the couch, "But Madison—"

"She's different," Murray cut him off, whipping his head around so fast to glare at Wayne, it almost made me to wonder if he was a vampire.

"Do I want to know how you know that?" I instinctively reached for my stakes, then sighed dejectedly.

Madison had my jacket, and my spare weapons were in my room on the far end of the apartment.

Wayne laughed and shook his head. "I've been known to camp out in the basement when I can't make it to more secure lodgings by sunrise. You kids aren't exactly quiet, and I have extremely good hearing."

Kids? He needs to quit calling people that. I'm thirty, and Murray is only a year younger than me. Then again, I had to remember Grandpa James-Dean-Reginald-Wayne was a vampire.

"Seriously, given what we do for a living, how the fuck did I not know about this?" I asked.

Wayne shook his head. "Because the few times I have visited, you were passed out in your underwear on the couch, and I didn't feel it appropriate to wake you," he said, earning himself a hard-earned glare from yours truly.

"What a night," I muttered. I didn't know what I meant by what I said. Was it because of my interactions with Madison, the carnage from the hotel, or that a vampire currently lounged on the couch where I normally sat? Maybe it was a combination of all of the above.

"Speaking of which, what happened at the party?" Murray asked.

I took the note with Ronald's handwriting from my back pocket and showed it to him. As he read the note, I explained what happened at the Phoenix, leaving out the bits about any awkwardness with Madison. His eyes immediately went wide with shock, his eyes transfixed on the note.

Murray looked up from the note and stared straight at me. "Holy shit! Apollo, after the vampires who killed

Ronald attacked, we had to run before the cops showed up. Do you think—"

"I don't know. If it was Ronald, I don't see how he could have caused all the carnage, and if he's been turned into a vampire, why would he ghost us for the past ten years?"

"It makes sense," Wayne said from the couch.

"You're not a part of this," I said, glaring at him.

Wayne sat up, and turned look at me. "Hey, this used to be my apartment," he said, shaking his head. "Anyway, like I said, it makes sense. When a vampire turns, certain parts of our personality become enhanced."

"Like your penchant for decades old fashion?" I quipped. Murray jabbed me in the arm with his fist. Ow, that hurt. Definitely not strong, which meant I only had to put up with one 'Vampire Murray' at the moment. "It still doesn't explain the bloodbath I walked into."

Murray tapped the paper in his hands against his fingers. "This note, he did like to pull pranks, and from what you've told me, it sounds like one hell of a party. My grandpa is right. Perhaps Ronald is a vampire, and maybe has something to do with Dr. Griffin's disappearance?" He paused as I rolled my eyes and left the kitchen "Apollo? Where are you going?" he asked.

"To sleep," I said, with more annoyance than originally intended. I had been hit with a Mack truck load of information I had to process, which required me to sleep and collect my thoughts. I was angry. Angry at the situation, my roommate, Wayne, Madison, Ronald, all of it.

"But it's night out," Murray protested.

I held up all the fingers on my right hand. "I'm tired," I said, lowering my thumb. "I'm cranky." My little finger came down next. "I smell bad," I brought down my ring finger, "and my best friend is possibly not as dead as I thought." I lowered my index, leaving my middle finger extended and fully pointed at Murray.

I exhaled slowly before continuing, "I'm going to Norman's tomorrow to get some more answers. I have a feeling he's been holding back."

My roommate exchanged glances with Wayne, who simply shrugged. "Fine, but be careful. Please don't cause a scene," Murray said.

Little did he know that's exactly what I intended to do. I ignored Murray's warning and stormed to my room, slamming the door behind me.

Norman went flying backward over his desk when my fist connected with his jaw. I didn't feel one damn bit sorry about it either. If it wasn't going to be for this, it would have been some other reason. The spindly bar owner got up, straightened his tie-dye shirt—I don't think I've ever seen him not wear one—and sat down in the chair behind the desk as if everything was perfectly calm and normal. What a pretentious little fuck.

I heard the distinct *pop* of bubblegum and glanced behind to see Tal standing in the doorway of Norman's, twirling a strand of the pink goo in her finger. Minus the elf ears, she wore her usual booty shorts and ass-kicker boots attire. She shrugged when she caught my gaze. Busting into Norman's office to beat the shit out of the man was par for the course.

"You can go, Tal," Norman wheezed, waving at the pint-sized bartender with a flip of his hand.

Tal continued playing with the bubblegum. "But I'm having so much fun watching you try to fly!" she exclaimed. The way she spoke forced me to suppress a snicker. Tal always had a way with making sarcasm sound cute.

"Now," he replied.

Tal rolled her eyes. "Fine," she said, drawing the word out as if she were a child putting on a show of defiance, then shoved the gum back in her mouth before leaving.

She closed the door behind her as she left, and I cast a sharp gaze back at Norman. "How the fuck could you have kept something like this from me?!" I shouted.

Norman raised an eyebrow. "I think, Mr. Grant, you're going to have to be more specific," he said.

I took a step toward the desk. "You knew Ronald was alive."

Norman shrugged, "I told you last time, you didn't want to get involved. You should've listened."

"You're a real piece of shit," I spat.

"I've been called worse."

I leaned past the desk, grabbing Norman by the collar and pulled him forward. "Give me one good reason not to kick the shit out of you again."

"What if I told you I know what the Coven wants Dr. Griffin for?" he asked, unfazed by the fact I had him in my grip.

"Why does that matter? They already have him. You said so yourself." I was practically growling at this point.

Norman looked at me with defiance. "Sit down and shut the fuck up, Mr. Grant."

I didn't feel like getting into a pissing contest with Norman, so I complied, releasing my hold and taking a seat in a rather uncomfortable metal folding chair. I'm almost positive from the groove in the seat it was used as a weapon at some point.

"Now that we've calmed down, let's talk about Dr.

Griffin," Norman said. It unsettled me how calm he kept his voice.

I started tapping my foot on the floor. My anger had to be redirected somewhere. "Make it quick, I'm running low on patience," I said.

Norman nodded. "You know how as vampires age, they don't immediately turn to dust when you kill them?"

Of course, I do, Dip-shit. You taught me that.

"Yeah, that only happens to the newly-turned," I said.

"If they get old enough, they can walk around in sunlight provided they've fed."

"That's in relation to the immortality curse, right?" I asked. A valid question. Very few people know how vampirism truly originated. The theories are varied. Some say it started as a disease, some say it's a curse. Hell, I'm willing to bet with being in Vegas someone probably thinks it's spread by contact with glitter. If that's the case, then Madison's shampoo had already turned me into an actual sexy version of Edward Cullen. *Nah, that can't be true. I would have combusted in the afternoon sun on the way over here.*

"Right," Norman said, breaking me out of my reverie.

Time to get back on topic. "What does this have to do with Dr. Griffin?" I asked.

Norman sighed, "I'm getting to that. I shouldn't be telling you this, but his family hails from a long line of witches."

"Just about everyone's family does at this point," I said. I mean, everybody knows somebody, who knows somebody, who knows some mother's sister's aunt who has a friend who reads tarot.

"Sure, okay, but are they all from the same line

responsible for creating the immortality curse?" Norman asked. I sensed a hint of disbelief in his response. He probably would have wrinkled his face, but his jaw continued to swell where I hit it. "Rumor has it our missing phlebotomist found a way to separate the curse from the blood. Do you know what this means?"

"Let me guess, some bad-ass vampire wants to create an army of super-vamps?"

"You're not entirely wrong," Norman said.

Okay, that got my attention. I might have purpose-fully been a sarcastic asshole, but I didn't think I'd actu-ally be right.

Norman continued, "Think of the ramifications if the powers granted by the curse were to go unchecked. A vampire with all of the strengths, but none of the weaknesses?"

My eyes went wide as I considered the possibilities. "Is that what Ronald's up to? Shit…"

"Mr. Grant,"

"Apollo," I corrected. I hated being called by my last name almost as much as Murray hated being called by his first.

"Mr. Grant," Norman pleaded, "Ronald is not the one you should be worried about."

"Come again?" I asked.

Norman took off his several layers of hemp bracelets and showed me his wrist. The newly exposed claw marks previously hidden underneath was unmistakable. Whoever was in control allowed Norman to tell me what he did and wanted me to know this information. No way it could have been Ronald. So, who the hell was screwing with me?

"The Coven captured the doctor but has so far been unable to figure out how to duplicate his results,"

Norman said. Almost a little too directly. I'm fairly certain at this point he was only telling me what whoever led the Coven wanted me to know. When I figure out who all is behind this, I'm going to give the mind-fucking piece of shit an ass-kicking which will turn them to dust, then I'll find a way to raise them from the dead so I can do it again.

For now, though, I decided to play along. I needed answers.

"You think that's why Connor got killed?" I asked.

Norman snorted, "No, that's exactly how the kid got killed."

Figured.

"Come again? What are you allowed to tell me? I know what those marks on your wrist mean." If I kept dropping gauntlets like this, I was going to have to ask Tal to keep them on special order behind the bar when I visited.

"The leader of the Coven wants the doctor's research found. I would suggest you and Murray locate it before they do."

"How do I know this isn't another trap?" Another valid question.

"You don't," Norman remarked, his voice firm.

But it most certainly is. Hopefully this one doesn't have as many dead bodies lying about. My ass felt numb as I stood up. Metal chairs and I don't get along. I left Norman's office, passed by the bar to wave at Tal, and exited without another word. I didn't know exactly where this missing research was, but I had a good idea of where to start looking.

Murray stood next to his car waiting for me in the parking lot. I didn't bother to question why he was there. Knowing him, he probably gave me some time to cool off before following me after I left for Norman's. I sighed. He needed to get an upgrade from a twenty-three-year-old clown car.

"Find out anything?" he asked.

"Not exactly." I opened up the Fiesta's back hatch door, took off the leather jacket and shoved it in the back. "The Coven wants our missing doctor to help them create an army of super-vamps. Not sure where Ronald fits in."

Murray *tsked*. "What do we do now?"

"How do you feel about laboratories?" I asked.

Murray simply looked at me and grinned.

7

A full day passed before we decided to visit Osiris Labs. This was the last place Dr. Griffin had been seen by the public, and I figured it would be as good a place as any to start our search. I squinted as Murray parked the car. This was the second day in a row I found myself working during the day and given the fact Osiris stood on the outskirts of Las Vegas in the Mojave Desert, the brightness outside nearly blinded me. I cursed not-so-silently about not bringing sunglasses when we exited the vehicle. Murray laughed quietly at my distress.

I wore a white lab coat instead of my usual leather, and its collar itched my skin. I scratched my neck and glanced at Murray as we walked toward the three-story building. He wore a similar coat. I sighed. The man could have at least used fabric softener when he ran these through the wash. He handed me a badge attached to a lanyard as we neared the entrance. It had been a while since we had to do undercover work.

"Did Wayne help you acquire these?" I put the lanyard over my neck. It swung as I moved.

"Believe it or not, I don't need my grandpa's help with everything," Murray glared at me.

I shook my head. It was going to take some time to get used to the relationship existing between him and Wayne, and even more to come to terms with the fact my roommate hid the truth about his grandfather being a vampire.

I opened the door to the entrance and followed Murray inside. He moved ahead of me to the receptionist desk. The girl working behind the counter had her blond hair pulled back in a tight braid. She looked up and gave us one of the most insincere smiles I had ever seen.

"Can I help you?" she asked, pursing her lips.

Murray showed the receptionist his badge. "We're here to inquire about Dr. Griffin."

I tuned the rest of what he said out as I turned to cross my arms and lean back against the desk. Murray and the receptionist engaged in a conversation of playful banter that made me wince. No, seriously, it was cringe-worthy listening to Murray flirt. I half expected him to slide a note across the counter with the words 'Do you like me, mark yes or no' written on it. *Someone remind me again how he ended up with Madison, please?*

"Hey, let's go," Murray said, grabbing my shoulder to get my attention. We walked over to a pair of elevators across the lobby.

"Where are we going?" I asked as Murray pressed the up arrow.

"It's on the third floor, Dr. Griffin's office. Margaret there was kind enough to hand me the key," Murray said. We heard the ding of the elevator and walked inside.

"I can't believe that shit you called flirting worked," I

said once the doors closed, squinting at Murray in disbelief.

"Stop complaining. I got what we need."

Looking around the lift cautiously as we went up, I said, "Hopefully this isn't another trap or dead end." Honestly, I didn't want the elevator to be stuck. Especially after the last time I had been in one.

Murray was about to respond when we arrived at the third floor. We stepped out into a large, well-lit room with small offices with their doors closed and shut blinds lining the walls. The main floor of the lab had individual workstations with projects I guessed by their appearance to be in various stages of progress. Most of the equipment in this room was foreign to me, but I did recognize a microscope and a centrifuge device. I guess watching forensic shows when nothing else is on TV did pay off. Maybe.

Murray nodded toward the back of the lab. "Let's go. Dr. Griffin's office is the big one in the back corner."

"Hey, Murray?" I huffed once we got to the office door. Murray walked fast, and I had to take long strides to keep up with him.

"Apollo?"

"Where is everyone?"

Murray shrugged. "It's six o'clock. Maybe they're at dinner?"

"Possibly," I said. "But let's keep an eye out. It's a little eerie." Didn't hurt to be careful.

Murray cast a downward glance as he used the key to open the door. "Seriously, Apollo. The sun hasn't gone down yet. I doubt any vampire would be here right now.

The hairs on the back of my neck relaxed, but I remained cautious as we entered Dr. Griffin's office. The tiny room had that old dusty book smell only people like

Murray seemed to enjoy. Personally, it gave me a headache. A small desk with a computer sat by a window.

Murray sat down at the desk and began fiddling with the machine. It made a strange whirr as it turned on. I guess the sound was normal. I stood by the window and looked through the blinds as he turned on the small desk lamp. Outside, the sun slowly began its descent.

"Apollo, be a dear and turn the blinds down for me, would you?" Murray asked.

"Whatever you say, Snookums." I jested, closing the blinds.

"You're a jerk." he said, tapping on the keyboard.

"You love me," I said with the sweetest of sarcasm, leaning forward to squeeze the side of Murray's cheek. I coughed as he hit me in the stomach, pushing me away.

"Only in the most platonic sense possible. You'd have to have a better set of tits and a rounder ass, and even then, I wouldn't consider it," Murray said.

I grinned. "The drive to California is only a matter of hours. I could get that fixed with a visit to a plastic surgeon in San Diego if you want."

Murray cast a glare in my direction. "No thanks," he said. I laughed.

"My feelings are hurt," I held a hand to my heart, pretending to be sad. "You know I'm kidding right? I mean, my ass is already perfect, and I'd make a horrible woman."

Murray shook his head. "Shut up, I'm trying to concentrate." There was a brief pause. "Cool. I'm in. The password was Connor's birthday," he said.

"Think you'll find what you are looking for in there?" I asked.

Murray's expression as he looked up at me said, *I*

know what the fuck I'm doing, and began poking around the files on the computer looking for Dr. Griffin's research. I find computers boring, so I walked back over to the door, and kept an eye on the lab, you know—just in case.

"Hmm…" Murray's voice trailed off.

I turned my head slightly back. "What's up?"

"I have a file here mentioning his work with the blood research, but there is this one labeled 'Lilith' I can't seem to open."

My curiosity was piqued. "Lilith? As in, first wife of biblical Adam?" I asked. Murray shot a curious glance at me. "What? I studied theology when I went to college."

Murray shrugged his shoulders. "Who knows? I'm going to copy the whole file onto my thumb drive and take it home with me. We don't want to stay here too long."

The hairs on the back of my neck suddenly rose to full attention. "A wise plan," I said.

A loud crash sounded from across the lab.

"Stay here," I cautioned. "I'm gonna go check whatever caused that noise."

I had a stake hidden in sheaths on the inside of each of my boots. I took them both out and tossed one to Murray.

"I'll keep working on this while you go take care of business."

Nodding, I closed the door behind me as I went to greet our newest arrival.

It didn't take much navigating my way through the lab stations before I found the source of the disturbance. I stepped in *something*. When I looked down, a string of entrails creeped along the floor, leading toward a copy room. I followed the trail of guts and other human parts, and had to steel myself for when I opened the copy room door. Let's just say, I knew where all the missing lab techs ended up, and leave it at that. Murray hadn't been entirely wrong about them being at dinner.

I kept my stake held in front of me when I heard a scream. Turning around, a woman in pink scrubs and a white lab coat ran past me. She didn't bother to glance in my direction as she ran by. She frantically pushed the down arrow on the elevator controls, and then her face froze in horror as a vampire appeared seemingly from out of nowhere, taking out a chunk of her neck before I made it over. Like, a literal chunk. The dude's hairy hands ripped her throat out, the blood dripping down his arm as her body fell to the floor

"You're gonna pay for that, asshole," I said once I got close. I got a good look of Hairy Hands as I approached. This vampire was one ugly mug. First, he wore glasses, which I found odd, but I've seen the undead wear weirder shit. The Hawaiian shirt was a bit outlandish, even for Vegas. The mop of shit on top of his head barely counting as hair appeared as if a cat tried to chew its own furball before coughing it back up. Normally, I'm not one to judge, but I was pretty sure Hairy Hands looked like this before he turned.

The vampire growled at me and lunged before I could strike. I fell back, dropping my stake, and landed in the forming pool of blood spreading from the woman's body. Gross. At least I had the lab coat on to keep my clothes from being completely ruined. I grabbed my stake as I stood up, quickly taking off the coat before the blood seeped through to my shirt. I dropped it on top of the dead woman and went running after Hairy Hands.

He paused right outside a door with a sign that said EMERGENCY STAIRWELL in big letters plastered on it. It felt like the letters were taunting me. Since I just witnessed him murdering a woman in front of me, I had no choice but to take the bait. Fucking bloodsucking asshole. I chased him down the windowless stairway to the bottom, and out the basement level door, which opened into a dank, moldy storage room.

Hairy Hands had disappeared.

I didn't have long to think about where he went, because he dropped down from behind me, and put me in a choke hold. The vampire's grip on my neck was tight, so I did the first thing that came to mind before I completely asphyxiated. I stabbed him in the leg with the stake. He loosened his hold just enough for me to deliver a backward elbow to his jaw. He staggered back. I pivoted quickly around, delivering a right hook to the asshole's face, and he fell to the ground. Vampires heal quickly, so before he stopped seeing stars, or whatever happened when vampires got clocked in the noggin, I pulled the stake out of his leg and drove it home straight into the vampire's heart.

"I served my purpose…" the vampire whispered before he died.

I discovered quickly he happened to be a much older vampire than those I'm used to fighting, and his lack of fashion sense may have been due to bad decision making. At least Wayne knew how to coordinate. Maybe he could've offered this guy some tips. The vampire didn't turn to dust, but rather, exploded in a spray of blood and guts that landed all over me. Gross. At least I didn't wear the leather jacket here.

What the hell did he mean, 'I served my purpose'? *Murray!*

I silently admonished myself for being distracted by Hairy Hands. Racing back upstairs to the top floor, I didn't bother to catch my breath, and huffed as I darted across the lab to Dr. Griffin's office.

Well, what was left of it anyway. The office had been trashed. Books and papers laid strewn about everywhere, and the computer previously sitting on the desk was missing.

I heard a soft moan coming from behind the desk. It was Murray. I found him beat to shit with trickles of blood running down his face. He had the stake I lent him clutched in his fist, and he was covered in vampire dust.

"Murray!" I knelt next to him.

"I tried to fight them off," he croaked. He let out a wheeze and coughed as I tried to sit him up.

"Fuck you, you little bitch, don't go dying on me now," I said.

Murray glared at me with his left eye. His right had swollen shut. "Trying…not to…" he muttered.

Sarcasm. Good. Sarcasm was good. It meant the injuries he sustained hadn't done any permanent damage. I think. Even with the bite marks on his neck. Fucking vampires.

"Did you drink?" I continued checking him for wounds. Thankfully, no claw marks. Surprising.

"Not that I can recall, I killed the vampire who bit me."

Good. Last thing I wanted to do was kill Murray. We agreed when we became hunters, if either of us ended up in a situation where we were bit and drank the blood of a vampire, we'd stake each other before we turned. I didn't want to do that now. Not today. Or ever if I wanted to be specific.

Murray attempted to stand and stumbled backward.

"Easy," I said, catching him before he fell. Due to the combination of being fed on and getting his ass handed to him, Murray was a tad on the light-headed side. I draped his arm over my shoulder. He leaned heavily for support as I helped him to stand.

"Give me your keys," I said.

"What?"

"Your keys. Give them to me. We're going home. I'm driving."

Murray looked up at me, concerned. However, I'm not the one with the fucked-up eye, covered in bruises, and bleeding from a cut to my face. After a moment, Murray dug in his pocket, took out his car keys, and pressed them into my hand.

We slowly took the stairs down. Given our present state of appearance, I hoped we'd find a service entrance to sneak out of in order to get back to the car without being noticed. We both looked like shit, and I desperately needed a shower.

8

We found the service entrance in the basement, and with the sun being down, a pair of vampires dressed like Hot Topic rejects with their hair in pigtails came racing toward us when we went outside. It was hard enough fighting these undead harlots off to begin with, never mind I was hampered by making sure Murray didn't collapse in the parking lot.

I managed to take them both out. Murray and I got in the car, and I drove off, but not before a group of vampires chased us out of the main entrance. I didn't have time for their undead bullshit. I drove the car unsteadily along the desert highway through the Mojave back toward Las Vegas proper. Most of my discomfort came from the fact I my legs barely fitted under the steering wheel of a car designed for a circus midget. I don't see how Murray managed to wedge himself daily behind the driver's seat.

Murray winced.

"It could be worse." We drove into the city proper.

"I just got my ass kicked, dude," Murray complained.

"I've been attacked and fed upon by vampires. They took the hard drive."

"Fuck." I didn't bother to shout. This newest development was another item on the long list of ways in which my life was being screwed by whomever enjoyed toying with me.

Murray reached gingerly into the pocket of his coat. It had been torn to shreds, but looked better than the blood-riddled mess I wore. He took out the thumb drive and wiggled it at me. "Hey, at least I got it backed up before they arrived," he said.

A wide smile spread across my face. "Snookums, I could kiss you right now."

"Whatever, Apollo. Let me get some painkillers in my system when we get home, and I might let you." Murray would have rolled his eyes if one didn't look like a grapefruit.

"Madison might get jealous," I snickered.

"Of you?" Murray asked.

"Maybe. I'm rather dashing," I said, putting on false airs.

We both laughed. I'm never telling him what happened with her at The Phoenix.

"I found something when I was copying the data over. I need to look into it when we get back." Murray paused and shifted his seatbelt as we approached a traffic light and stopped. "You're not going to like it."

Of course. Here comes the next item on the list of fuckery. *What now,* I wondered. "Just like I don't enjoy that some unknown player is yanking my chain, dragging me all over the city to do their dirty work?" I turned my head to look at Murray. "Dr. Griffin is under the control of the Coven, his research is gone, and then there is the issue with Ronald…how the hell does he fit into all of this? "

Murray sighed, "Apollo, will you shut the fuck up and listen?!"

I didn't realize the windows were down or I never turned on the radio, until a decent looking family—likely tourists from the plainness of their clothing—walked past, steering their two small children immediately in the opposite direction. The father turned back and stared at us for a moment as the mother frantically tried to cover both of her children's ears. I raised an eyebrow. I mean, c'mon, you're in Vegas. Sin City. You knew what you were getting into when you showed up here. If one little F-bomb is going to bother you, maybe you should make better choices concerning your travel plans.

Catching a glimpse in the mirror, I realized it probably wasn't Murray's use of the profanity that caught their attention, but rather the car looked like a rolling crime scene unit, except without the chalk outlines and some rookie cop pocketing a hidden bag of cannabis to smoke later.

Settling back in my seat, I leaned my head back. I pretended to, anyway. The tiny interior only had so much room. "Fine, talk."

"It's about what I saw. Most of the records I caught a glimpse of indicated Dr. Griffin had been successful in his original experiment separating a vampire from the blood-curse, but he's only been able to do it once so far. 'Project Lilith', it said in his notes."

That piqued my curiosity. "You think whoever this vampire he tested his process on is the one leading the Coven?"

Murray nodded. "I'm willing to bet on it."

"Do we know who 'Lilith' is?"

"I'm not certain. I wasn't able to crack the contents of the Lilith file. I only looked at basic reports. I'm going to see if I can dig into it when we get home." Murray grunted as he shifted in his seat again.

The honk of the angry driver behind us gave me a start. When did the light turn green? I floored it. As fast as you could push pedal to the metal in a Ford Fiesta. Which wasn't very fast, by the way. Murray put the thumb drive back in his pocket, and we drove the rest of the way home in silence.

"Do I want to know what happened?" Wayne asked as I helped Murray into the apartment. The vampire sat on the floor in front of the coffee table. At this point, shit had gone so wrong with everything, I didn't even care a bloodsucker was lounging in the place.

Murray looked at Wayne with his good eye. "You see, what had happened was——"

Wayne raised a hand. "No, never mind, I don't want to know. It was probably Apollo's fault."

"The fuck it was!" I muttered.

Murray let me go and stumbled into the kitchen, grabbing an ice pack from the freezer before walking back into the living room. The flush of a toilet sounded and Madison came out of the bathroom. I gulped. The neon pink crop top and form fitting blue jeans she had on left very little to the imagination.

"Babe, are you okay?!" Madison shouted, rushing over to Murray's side. She punched me in the arm. "What did you do to him?" she asked.

I took a step back, not wanting to get hit again. "It wasn't my fault," I said.

"Totally was his fault," Murray said, grinning at me. If he was going to be this kind of sarcastic after getting his ass handed to him in a vampire fight, I'm going to have to start leaving him at home.

"Ha, I knew it!"

"Stay out of this, Wayne!" I snapped. Wayne chuckled then turned his attention to the tile-based board game laid out on the coffee table.

"Madison, stop. I'll be fine," Murray protested, pushing the woman's hands away from his face as she attempted to check his injuries.

Madison wrinkled her nose. "You look like shit, both of you. Apollo, you reek," she said, holding her hand briefly in front of her nose.

"Really? I hadn't noticed." I took off my shirt and tossed the vampire blood-covered mess on the floor. "Here, is that better?" I asked. Madison and Murray groaned audibly. I laughed, then picked up the shirt and threw it away in the kitchen garbage.

Murray grabbed Madison's hands and placed them at her side. "Seriously, quit. I'm going to go shower, then get back to work. I have research to do."

"You need to rest," Madison cautioned.

"I said I'll be fine," Murray argued as he stomped toward the bathroom.

Madison pouted, and it nearly made my heart melt. *Stop it, she's not yours,* I thought. I needed a shower, but Murray pretty much already called dibs, so I followed her into the living room and sat on the couch while she sat on the opposite side of the table from Wayne. Apparently, we had arrived home in the middle of a Carcassonne game.

I sighed, remembering the day Ronald had taught the game to me when I went to college. Carcassonne consisted of tiles, and people pieces called meeples. The objective was to place the tiles, build cities, roads, and farms using said tiles the meeples were placed on, then score points based on their positioning. I enjoyed the game, but I was horrible at it.

As I watched the two place tiles in turn, I tried to come to terms with the oddity of a vampire and a super-hot Vegas showgirl playing board games in my apartment. Wayne had a lead on the scoreboard, but Madison was probably going to beat him with weird farmer meeple scoring at the game's end.

"Wayne, before we took a break, you were telling me about your first day as a vampire?" Madison asked, placing a tile on the table.

"Night actually, but yes," Wayne said.

"Semantics," I muttered.

Wayne glared at me, then continued, "Anyway, it was…odd. That evening I woke up with nausea, and a headache I couldn't explain. I was blood-starved, and hadn't told anyone I had been turned into a vampire. I got dressed, and somehow wound up at a party I don't ever remember being invited to hosted by a dude named Nick. He had this personal casino in his basement, and when I introduced myself, he made a pun about the moon waxing and waning. I ignored him and the rest of his annoying ass jokes and took my place at the craps table. I found it both amusing and annoying he had one considering the amount of shit he talked for most of the event.

"Later in the evening, Nick is like, 'Okay guys, remember, the stakes are high'. That's when I lost it. The rage built inside of me. Next thing I know, I drank him and everyone in the room dry. Once I calmed down and stared at the bodies lying dead around the table, I realized he was talking about prize money, and it had nothing to do with me being a vampire. As I mentioned before, my newly acquired member of the undead status hadn't been revealed yet. Also, my wife was in the hospital about to have our baby."

"Murray's dad, right?" Madison asked.

"Mm hmm. Reginald Jr." Wayne placed the last tile in the game, and I watched as he began to calculate the final score. "My grandson is Reginald Wayne Murray III."

The Third? That was something I didn't know. I doubled over on the couch, and shamelessly cried from laughing so hard. Murray is never going to hear the end of me calling him Reginald now. Never fucking ever.

Madison punched me in the arm, quickly bringing me to my senses. Wayne looked sullen, then said. "One hundred and fifty points, Damn, girl."

"What can I say? Murray's an excellent teacher," Madison said.

"Good game," he complimented.

"Of course, and I can't wait to hear the rest of the story."

Neither can I, I thought. I heard doors slamming behind me. Murray must be done with the bathroom. Madison giggled as she helped Wayne put the game pieces back in the box.

"Some other time. I need to get going," Wayne said. "Regaling you with my story reminded me I'm hungry."

I slowly raised a cautious eyebrow.

"Don't look at me like that, Team Jacob," the vampire quipped. Grandpa Wayne's got jokes. How the fuck am I going to handle having two Murrays in my life? "I'm a vampire, I need to feed. Don't worry, I only feed on the tourists, and never enough to cause any permanent harm. I'm not that kind of monster anymore," he said. Wayne ran with vamp-speed out of the apartment, leaving me and Madison alone.

Madison stood up and leaned back as she stretched. The platform sandals she wore put her belly button right in front of my nose. Thankfully, she stepped away before my manhood and I had a question of ethics as to where exactly the line was on my moral compass.

"I should probably be going home too," she yawned. "Not much to do since the show is canceled." Madison was here at our apartment so much I forgot she had her own abode six blocks away.

"You're not staying here? I'm sure Murray would enjoy your company," I said.

Madison shook her head. "No, even with that eye, he has research-face. I want to sleep, which I can't do if he's tapping away on his damn keyboard."

"I'll see you out," I said, standing up from the couch.

Madison spun around to face me right as we got to the door, and I nearly stumbled into her. "Care to walk me home?" she asked.

"I—"

I probably shouldn't, is what I should have said. Instead, I stood there like a teenage boy getting his first boner. No seriously. Little Apollo had no problems stating his opinions right at that moment.

"Please?" Madison blinked in a way that was a cross between innocence and 'come hither'.

What the fuck? A little walk isn't going to hurt. Murray would appreciate me seeing Madison gets home safely. At least that's the lie I kept telling myself as I put on a black hoodie hanging by the door and zipped it up, then followed Madison out of the apartment.

9

Storm clouds rolled in, blocking my view of the twinkling desert sky as I walked Madison home. Not that I would have seen much of it anyway. Granted, she didn't live on the Strip, but there were enough buildings with neon signs and florescent lights implying an active nightlife in this part of town.

We turned a corner. There were no streetlights or welcoming storefronts. It might as well have been a den of crime. From the way a group of homeless men sitting next to a boarded-up bookstore we passed catcalled Madison, the street we were on probably was.

"Thanks for coming along, Apollo," Madison said, holding onto my arm as we walked down the darkened street.

"Sure thing, Murray would probably kick my ass if I let you walk alone in this," I said. She held her hand in front of her mouth as she giggled, and I felt sweat pooling in the back of my neck. Granted, her reaction was part of her normally unpredictable behavior, but damn, I had a hard as hell time keeping it together. *Cool it, all I need to do is get her home, then walk back. That's it.*

Even in the darkness, Madison stood close enough to me I could admire her visage. Granted, her attire was nothing like our previous rendezvous, but the clothing hugged her in quite an enticing manner. From the way she smiled, I'm pretty sure she remained aware of how she looked.

Before I entertained any more thoughts about Madison, her clothing, or sometimes lack thereof, the bottom of the sky fell out in a torrential downpour of rain.

"C'mon!" Madison grabbed my hand and practically dragged me the remaining two blocks to her apartment building. How she didn't fall over in those platform heels, I'll never guess, I was too busy trying not to focus on her nipples that were playing peekaboo from beneath her top.

"Let's get inside," she said once we got to the building's entrance, which thankfully had a small awning hanging overhead. She took a keycard out of her back pocket, swiped it at the access panel, and held the front door open. "Are you coming or not?"

My dumb idiot ass stood silently underneath the awning. I didn't care to walk home in a torrential downpour, so I followed the woman inside. The elevator took us to floor fifteen without incident. My heart raced as she led me down the hallway to her apartment. I shouldn't be this nervous. The woman simply happened to be offering me shelter from the storm. She unlocked the door to her unit, and I followed her inside.

"I'll be right back," Madison said.

I watched as she walked briskly to what I assumed was the bathroom.

"Damn," I said breathlessly, taking a moment to

examine the place. The difference between the living area above the Queen's Pawn and her apartment was night and day. White walls, matching black and maroon décor, and an electric fireplace with a gorgeous painting of a sunset hanging above it. I ran my hand across the throw pillow on the couch and noticed it had a silk cover. Nice silk, not that cheap shit you find at department stores. I glanced down the hallway to the open door of the bedroom and briefly wondered if the sheets were made of silk also. *Get your mind out of the gutter.*

I walked around the living room. In the back were a pair of giant glass windows which slid open to a small balcony. The view of the Las Vegas skyline here was spectacular. Or would have been if there wasn't a torrential thunderstorm outside. Madison apparently had a taste for the fine and extravagant, so why the hell did she spend most of her time with losers like Murray and myself?

"Hey," Madison said. Her tap on my shoulder caused me to nearly jump.

"I'm sorry?" I asked, turning to face her.

"I'm not going to have you in here while there's a thunderstorm outside and you smell like—" Madison motioned to the bloodstains on my pant leg "—whatever you guys fought earlier today. Take a fucking shower, and I'll go see if I have any dry clothes of Murray's here which might actually fit you. I left a towel and a fresh bar of soap on the counter."

"Are you going to join me?" I quipped.

"Not even in the wildest of your wet dreams," Madison retorted.

I feigned being shocked. "Harsh."

Madison shook her head. "Honest. Now go clean up. You stink."

I sniffed the air, confirming Madison's assessment of my hygiene. I did reek. And I doubt being caught in the rainstorm outside helped any. I couldn't have protested her request even if I wanted to. She pushed me into the bathroom and closed the door behind me once I entered. Looking forward to being clean and not covered in vampire shit, I stripped naked.

I hung the towel on the door of the shower stall before stepping inside and turned on the faucet. Immediately, I smiled. The best thing about the bathroom was the water coming out of the showerhead at a perfect just-warmer-than-lukewarm temperature. *Holy shit, this is nice.* I slid the door to the stall closed. I placed the soap bar in an empty shelf on the shower caddy in the wall and saw a bottle of shampoo sitting there. Curious, I squirted some of the shampoo into my hand, grateful it didn't contain glitter.

Then, the shower door opened, and this time, I did jump. Madison casually stepped inside, closing the door to the stall behind her—and not wearing a stitch of anything other than the locks of raven-dark hair gently caressing the sides of her breasts. Holy fucking shit to all hell, I was screwed.

"You know, I think I might have changed my mind," she whispered softly. I don't recall much from the next few moments because her hand gingerly brushed past my ear as she kissed me gently on the neck, and I lost all control, giving into her advance. Her legs wrapped around my waist as she held onto my shoulders while I gripped her thighs, pressing her body tightly against the back wall of the shower as I went into her. Many, many times.

Let's just say after we were done in the shower, I'm

now definitely able to confirm the sheets on Madison's bed were made of some incredibly luxurious silk.

———

Light from the morning sun came in through the bedroom window, forcing me awake. I narrowed my eyes. If waking up in the daylight ended up becoming my new normal, I might have to start considering taking on a new profession. Yawning, I shifted underneath the silken sheets of Madison's bed, turning over to find the woman absent. A small note was left lying in the impression of the pillow where Madison's head used to be.

Picking up the note, I read aloud, "You were passed out, and I couldn't wake you. I have to go take care of a few errands. Please see yourself out."

Crumpling up the paper, I laid back and stared at the ceiling. I felt a little light-headed, but nothing out of the ordinary. What a fucking night. Literally.

I turned my head and saw my clothes folded in a chair in the corner. Madison must've put them there. I slid out of bed and put on my pants. As I reached for my hoodie, my cell phone rang. Good thing to know it didn't get damaged while I was caught in last night's storm.

I pulled the device out of my back pocket and sat on the edge of the bed. Thankfully, due to the extended battery, it had a charge. When the name displayed on the caller ID, I winced. Murray's name flashed in bright white letters. Shit. This conversation had the possibility of being worse than the walk of shame I was about to take back home. Thankfully, the phone hung up before I could answer. Dodging a bullet is always a positive. I laced up my boots, and the phone rang again.

I sighed dejectedly before answering the call.

"Hello," I said.

"Apollo, where are you?!" Murray shouted. He sounded frantic.

"Held up at a beautiful woman's home where she savagely ravished my body until the wee hours of the morning." Only a smidgeon of what I said had some truth to it. Madison and I were invested equally in last night's engagement. I wasn't ready for the ramifications of telling my roommate I had some of the best sex of my life with his girlfriend.

Murray scoffed, "Right, whatever, you can tell me the true story when you get here—"

Never going to happen.

"How close are you to home?" He asked.

"Probably thirty minutes, why?" I asked. In all reality, it would only take me minutes to walk the six blocks back home, but I needed to buy myself some more time.

"Just get here when you can. I managed to crack open the Lilith file."

"Oh yeah?"

"Mm hmm. All the details from Dr. Griffin's experiments were in there. How he did it, why he did it," There was a short pause before Murray continued, "I know who Dr. Griffin used as his original test subject. You're not going to believe—"

A sound of a loud crash interrupted Murray.

"What the fuck are you doing here?!" Murray exclaimed. I heard a cacophony of noises like the apartment was being ripped asunder while Murray was in a physical altercation.

"Fuck you, man. Let me go!" Murray cried.

"Murray? Murray?!" My heart raced. "Who's there with you?!"

The phone disconnected. Fuck.

"Murray!" I shouted. What the fuck had happened? What danger had Murray gotten himself into? I might've broken some non-existent bro-code for screwing around with Madison, but I still cared about the man. I quickly put on my hoodie and rushed out of Madison's apartment, racing toward home.

I hoped I got there in time.

10

My fears were confirmed as soon as I got home. Or, what remained of it anyway. The front door had been ripped off its hinges, and now laid in the center of the living room floor. Shreds of fluff strewn about was all that had been left of Murray's couch. The place had been completely ransacked, everything in my line of sight either torn askew or broken.

"Murray?!" I called out but got nothing in reply.

"He's not here," Wayne said quietly as he poked his head out of Murray's bedroom.

"Wayne, what the fuck are you doing here?" I asked. "It's the middle of the damned morning!"

Wayne narrowed his eyes. "Notice how I'm confined to the hallway, and not in the living room? I came back last night after you left and crashed on the couch. Some asshole busted in here and took my grandson and his computer stuff, but left the curtains open so I'm stuck."

"Speaking of which, where is Murray?" I looked around at what was left of the apartment.

"I would love to know the answer myself, but first, can you close those curtains?" he asked.

I snorted. "How do I know you didn't cause all this?"

Grandpa Vampire glared at me. "Would I be here if I were to blame?"

He had a point. I sighed, then closed the curtains to the living room window. Wayne stepped out from Murray's bedroom and walked into the kitchen. He had sustained some cuts to his face, but they were rapidly healing.

"What the hell happened here?"

"Right when Murray called you, some vampire dressed in protective black gear came in here and opened the curtains. We fought for a bit, and he knocked me out."

"Did you recognize him?"

Wayne shook his head. "No, but I'm pretty sure he's the one who took Reggie."

I didn't bother to suppress my laughter. "Reggie?"

Wayne scowled at me. "Don't laugh. He's my grandson. I can call him what I want." He propped himself against kitchen counter. "There is something I realized when I came to. Something you should know."

"I'm listening."

"I've been keeping a watch over my family for decades. I might be a vampire, but this shop, this place, I have a connection to it. Even after that vamp demoness turned me into what you see before you."

"Where is this going, old man?" I asked impatiently.

"Shut up and listen." Wayne might look similar to my age, but his tone carried a sense of authority that comes with those belonging to an older generation. He continued, "I didn't realize it before until the other night, Apollo. She's strong, you'll need to be careful."

I didn't like where this was going. "Who?"

Wayne sighed, "Madison, your roommate's girl-friend. It came back to me after I came to."

I felt like the gut feeling in my stomach started filling with bile. "Impossible. There is no way Madison did any of this," I said.

"Not this mess, you idiot. She's the vampire who turned me."

I blinked my eyes in disbelief and leaned forward. "I'm sorry, you want to repeat that one more time? I could've sworn you said Madison is the vampire who turned you."

Wayne simply nodded. "I saw when Reggie opened the file. It was all there in his notes. Madison was Dr. Griffin's original test subject. Madison—"

"—is Lilith." I finished. It didn't take much for me to connect the dots. Madison Lily. Lily. Lilith. It made a shit-ton of sense even if I didn't want it to. All the pleasure and everything I experienced from the night before instantly drained away. *How long has this fucking bitch been playing me?* I wanted to puke. In fact, I rushed over to the garbage can in the kitchen and did.

Wayne patted me on the shoulder as I stood back up. "Are you okay?"

No, you asshole, I just had sex with my best friend's girlfriend, who, it turns out, is actually a vampire. "If you know this, why didn't you tell me before?" I asked instead.

"The mark she put on me." Wayne showed his wrist to me. "It's worn off. She's been playing us."

"No fucking shit." Now I had to deal with Madison being a vampire, her identity as Lilith, as well as being the culprit behind all the shit that's gone wrong over the past several days. What the ever-loving fuck? "This has to be a fucking joke."

Never mind Madison has fucked me in more ways than one.

"I can assure you it's not," Wayne said as I walked down the hallway. "Where are you going?"

"I need a minute," I said. Stumbling toward the bathroom. I gripped the sink hard as I looked at myself in the mirror. Everything Wayne said had made sense, but I didn't want to believe it. Madison, a vampire. Knowing my luck, she's probably the current leader of the Coven also. Looking up, I took notice of my haggard reflection in the mirror. Then, I saw something I didn't want to see. I pulled the collar of my hoodie down and growled. Like a fucking dog in a pit fight growl. On the side of my neck were two very tiny puncture marks. Dammit, Madison.

"Holy shit," Wayne whispered. I didn't even realize I had left the door open.

"She fucking bit me," I muttered.

"Apollo, I bite people. I'm talking about this—"

"What the fuck are you doing?" Wayne pulled my hand up and placed it on the back of my neck. Never mind the bite marks, as soon as I felt the indentations from being scratched, I became pissed. There was being played, then there was this. Fucking hell.

I didn't bother stopping to listen to Wayne's protest as I stormed past him and marched back to my room. I was tired, pissed off, light-headed, cranky, and needed to change clothes. What shocked me when I opened the room was it hadn't been touched. Even more surprising, were the two playing cards lying on my pillow. A jack and an ace of spades. A winning blackjack combo.

Without question, I already knew who took Murray.

I had nothing to do for the rest of the day but wait. Don't get me wrong, I wanted to go save Murray, find Madison and drive a stake through her heart, and figure out how the hell Ronald figured into everything, but reason got the better of me. Well, not so much reason, but rather Wayne's sucker punch to my face which brought me to my senses. It would be unwise to rush in blindly. In order to succeed at whatever came next, I would need help. And what help would be better than an equally pissed off vampire who has the same goals as me?

I looked in my closet mirror and rubbed my cheek. The red spot on the side of my face was going to be one hell of a shiner.

I turned around to face Wayne. He sat on the edge of my bed, staring at me. "Shit, did you have to hit me so hard?" I asked.

"That's what you get for trying to run out of here half-cocked," Wayne replied. I don't know what was worse, that he had changed into black T-shirt and ripped jeans I was certain came out of Murray's wardrobe, or that he looked at me with a shit-eating grin. "Look, I want to save Reggie as much as you do, but we have to be smart about this."

I scowled at Wayne, then searched the bottom of my closet for my weapons.

"What?" he asked, almost a little too innocently.

"Look, just because you may be right, doesn't mean I'm fully ready for this to turn into a buddy-cop situation."

"Heh," Wayne laughed.

Where the fuck was the bag with all my weapons in it? "Shit!" I exclaimed.

"What's wrong?"

"Everything's gone," I said. "Ronald isn't stupid. He left those cards as a message, but he took all the weapons. The stakes, the silver chains, gone."

I stood up and ran a hand through my hair as I pondered what to do. Besides my charming good looks and personality, I wasn't going to go hunting after Madison and who knows what else from the Coven without at least one stake.

Wayne shrugged. "That sucks."

"Vampires suck."

"We do."

I laughed. "Be glad the only reason I haven't killed you yet is because of Murray."

Wayne nodded. "I can live with that."

"But, you're not—" Wayne raised an eyebrow at me. "—never mind," I said, shaking my head. I wasn't going to argue semantics with someone who has lived generations longer than me.

"Where are you going?"

"Don't worry, I'm not going to be stupid. I'm going to see if I can fix the door, so you aren't stuck in the back of the apartment all day." If Murray made it out of this, I didn't want to add 'I burned your vampire grandfather to dust' to my list of offenses.

Wayne stood in the hallway while I picked up the door to the apartment. So much for that plan. The hinge had been torn clean off. I propped the door up in what was left of the doorway. "Wayne, do me a favor," I said. "Murray keeps a roll of duct tape on his bedpost. Would you be kind enough to toss it to me?"

"Sure, but why would my grandson keep it...oh..." Watching Wayne realize the kind of kinky shit Murray and Madison were into amused me.

I laughed. "Imagine having to listen to those two

every night she stayed over." Never mind my experience with Madison was just as intense without the duct tape. I tried not to dwell on it. I almost felt guilty for not feeling guilty. I enjoyed our little soiree.

Why the fuck didn't I see it?

"See what?" Wayne asked. I realized I voiced my thought aloud. Wayne tossed me the tape, and I began tearing strips of it to secure the door to the doorway. I only needed it to last until the sun went down. I didn't want my back-up partner to accidentally wander out here and catch on fire.

"Madison—Lilith, whatever her name is," I said.

"She's strong. She probably had some kind of power over you. And by the look on your face, I'm guessing she didn't need to enthrall you before she gave you those scratches on your neck to do it." Wayne crossed his arms and sat on the pile of fluff that used to be the couch.

I finished taping the door in place. "Can you blame me? She might be an evil bitch, but she's one hot evil bitch."

"You're not wrong," Wayne smirked. "She looked exactly the same when she turned me almost sixty years ago."

I turned to face the vampire. "And you're only now remembering this?"

Wayne shrugged. "She compelled me to forget. Lilith does it to everyone she turns. I started to remember after she had me tell the story of my first night as a vampire."

"But why you?" I asked.

"Who knows? Maybe she was bored, or just plain hungry. I didn't see her much after that night, until about a few years ago, when she sent some of those Coven vamps after your friend Ronald."

I closed my eyes and winced. The dots finally started

connecting. Ronald, saving Madison, Dr. Griffin, Connor, Norman, meeting Wayne, the party at the Phoenix, the incident at the lab, the night at her apartment, Murray—it was all one large elaborate scheme. I had been played for a fool, and fell for her ruse hook, line, and sinker. Props to Lilith for playing the long game, but now I was pissed.

"You okay, Apollo?"

"Fuck no. She's had her seductive little fingers in my business ever since I arrived in Vegas, and now is going to pay for it. I am curious about something though. How did she know to seek out Dr. Griffin or learn about his research in the first place?"

Wayne shook his head. "Unfortunately, I don't know the answer to that one. Know anyone who might?"

"As a matter of fact, I do," I said, "and as soon as the sun goes down, we're going to a bar."

Murray's car keys were in the kitchen, so Wayne and I took the Fiesta to Norman's. I smiled when I spotted a leather jacket and a couple of stakes in the back seat.

The parking lot was empty when we arrived, save for Lars guarding the front door.

Lars placed one of his hammer sized hands onto my chest and pushed me back. It surprised me the man didn't fold me in half.

"You can't go inside," he said in a low, gravelly tone.

"What the hell do you mean?"

Shit was about to get real. Norman might be under the influence of a she-devil, but entering the bar had never been an issue before.

Wayne stepped in front of me. "I got this."

He made the mistake of taking an unwelcome step toward Lars.

I didn't think vampires could fly until the bouncer's punch sent Wayne soaring backward through the air, crashing into the roof of Murray's car. Wayne laid in a daze, either seeing whatever vampires saw as stars, or legitimately the stars twinkling down from the nighttime sky. I knew about Lars' strength from personal experience, but damn.

"He's not here," Lars said.

I shook my head. "Impossible, Norman is always here."

Lars remained vigilant and crossed his arms. "Not today, bar is closed."

"Then there's no need for you to be guarding the door, is there, sweet cheeks?" I asked with a grin.

Lars growled as he locked stares with me, forcing me to take a step back. I gulped. If memory served me correctly, this was the start of how I ended up with a broken arm the last time Lars and I had a conversation.

Wayne lunged straight at the man's waist, tackling him to the ground. I watched with amazement as they duked it out in a bout of fists and punches. To be honest, Lars made me jealous, and I wondered briefly why he wasn't part of the monster hunting game. Eventually, Wayne's face turned into its less-amicable form as he pinned Lars to the pavement.

"Stop. That is enough."

The firm tone of Tal's voice from behind me stopped Wayne from pursuing any further course of action. Turning around, I faced the woman as she leaned against the entrance to the building. She didn't look pleased.

"Apollo, bring your vampire friend and come with

me," she said. "And Lars, when you dust off your wounded pride, stay at the door. No one else comes in this time—I mean it."

"Yes, ma'am," Lars said quietly, his breath labored due to the strength of the vampire pinning him down.

Wayne stared at me, confused and I shrugged. He stood up and offered a hand to Lars, who obviously declined, standing up on his own. Wayne and Lars stared at each other in mutual understanding that there was a cease-fire.

"You boys coming, or not?" Tal held the door open.

Wayne and I nodded, then followed her inside.

I thought my apartment had been trashed, but the devastation here topped that mess. Tables and chairs tossed askew; décor torn off the walls. The stage in the back, destroyed. The only part of the bar which actually look like it survived whatever the hell happened was the actual bar.

"Sit, both of you. He'll be out in a moment." Tal grabbed a bottle of whiskey from behind the counter and pour a shot for me and Wayne. "On the house."

"Thanks," we both said, before taking our drinks in unison.

The sound of a door slamming came from the hallway behind the bar, and Norman stumbled out. I thought I was going to have a bruise on my face where Wayne punched me, but as beat up as he looked, this guy might end up needing a whole new face. The dude could seriously have passed for a *Walking Dead* extra without any additional makeup.

"You look like regurgitated dog shit," I said.

"Good to see you too, Apollo," Norman grunted, taking a seat at the far end of the bar. Tal slid another shot of whiskey his way. "If it makes you feel any better, I got my ass kicked for helping you out."

"Really?" I asked, "I thought you were under—"

"The control of an elder vampire? One as ancient as say…someone named Lilith?"

"Did you say ancient?" I felt gross. On second thought, I wouldn't mind tapping a good-looking cougar or two.

Norman nodded. "She's probably one of the oldest known alive, probably thousands of years or so. She never told me exactly, not that I would ask. Can't compel someone to forget what you don't tell them."

Wayne tilted his head. "He makes a valid point."

I spun around in my stool and leaned back against the bar, turning my head to address Norman. "You're telling me the enchantment or whatever she put on you wore off, and you're having a sudden moment of clarity?"

"And a shit-ton of regret," Norman said. "That temptress had control of me for years and only allowed me to tell you what she wanted you to know. Lilith is incredibly patient and enjoys playing the long game."

"It doesn't make any sense."

"Ancient vampire, Apollo," Norman replied, shaking his glass up in the air.

Tal gave a thin-lipped smile as she walked over and filled it with another shot of whiskey.

"If she's so old, she should be able to do what other ancient vampires do, you know, feed, walk in sunlight…"

"Maybe she wanted to do such without the need to feed," Wayne said. "I know I sure as hell would. Immortality sucks when you accidentally kill your friends because you're feeling a bit peckish."

"Exactly, it's why she sought out Dr. Griffin upon

learning about his research and his family lineage. She figured if she separated herself from the blood-curse, then she'd be able to do the same thing for other vampires and create an army loyal to her without using any form of enchantment."

"You boys need to be careful if you're going after her. For a vampire as strong and as old as she is, this is simply the next step in her game."

"Careful is my middle name," I quipped.

"If that isn't the biggest crock of shit...but no, seriously," Norman cautioned. "Keep your wits about you. You guys need to stop her, or I won't be able to maintain this bar. I can't keep having it trashed every time some evil upstart wants to become the next supernatural prime evil."

"How did you manage to fight off whatever attacked here?"

"I didn't," Norman replied.

"I did," Tal said, sliding another round of shots toward all of us.

I raised an eyebrow. "Come again?" I could literally carry her with one hand over my shoulder. Something about the angle of her smile told me if I did though, things would end poorly for me, and a broken arm received from Lars would feel fantastic in comparison.

"I'm stronger than I look, Sparkles," Tal giggled.

Wayne slapped his hand on the bar as he busted out in laughter.

"You are never going to let that go, are you?"

"Nope, never." Tal said, winking at me. "Oh, and our visitors earlier left this on the counter, I think they actually left it for you." Tal took out a postcard and handed it to me. I sighed as soon as I looked at the picture, knowing exactly what it meant.

"What is it?" Wayne asked.

"Another trap," I groaned.

The postcard had a picture of the Eiffel Tower on the front. On the back was written three words unmistakably in Ronald's handwriting—*Blackjack and Hookers.*

11

Okay, *Ronald, where the fuck are you?* Leaning back against one of the Paris' familiar slot machines, I enjoyed my view of the girls dancing around the poles in the middle of the blackjack tables. Here's to hoping I wouldn't get anyone killed. But given the previous few days, I wasn't banking on it.

Wayne had wandered off to scout the casino floor after I told him what Ronald looked like. The crowds were especially thick tonight. I straightened the collar of my jacket and sighed. The message on the postcard my formerly dead best friend left with Tal had been perfectly clear. I arrived at the place he wanted me to be, so now what?

"Dammit Ronald, I don't have time for this!" I muttered.

Wayne approached me, hands on his hips and shaking his head. "No luck, I can't find him."

I rolled my eyes. "What a surprise." I said dryly. "Another diversion, another trap. What I'm trying to figure out is why here—" Then it hit me. This was where

I spotted Connor with the lady vamp several days ago. Lilith had been using Ronald the entire fucking time, and he saw it all go down. Fuck. He probably called the cops on me too. I took a quick look around the casino floor.

So, he would have to be standing…

"Hey Apollo, I think we're being watched."

Wayne pointed at the slot machine. I saw his reflection, and further back….*No fucking way.* I spun around, but Ronald had disappeared. A group of confused gamblers nearby gave me the stink-eye.

"Apollo!" Wayne shouted, pointing at the back of Ronald's curly-haired head in the distance. I took a moment to process before giving chase. After all, I hadn't seen the man since I thought him dead. We followed Ronald as he weaved his way through the casino toward the hotel entrance. Hotel patrons and staff jumped out of our way as we ran to catch up to him. As we exited the Paris's hotel doors I gasped for breath as I caught sight of Ronald slipping into a cab. As the cab drove off, a flyer for *Illumination* flittered through the air and landed on my feet. I knew where we had to go next.

"Let's go," I said.

"Do we follow?"

I nodded. "We have to."

This was par for the course. Receive invitation, fall into trap. With the possibility of Murray's life on the line, this better be the end of this fucking nonsense, or there would be hell to pay.

Wayne ran a hand through his slicked-back hair. "Why lead us here if the destination is somewhere else?"

"Because, it's like Norman told us," I began, "Lilith is playing the long game. She's toying with us." *And me especially.* "Now, let's go save Murray and hopefully the world while we're at it."

"Sounds like a fun Saturday night," Wayne laughed.

I blinked at him for a moment. Pulling out my phone, I requested an Uber. Five minutes later, we were in a car and on our way to the Phoenix.

Wayne and I shared confused glances as we walked into the Phoenix. From the way everyone carried on, you would never have guessed an epic massacre had occurred on the top floor of the building only a few nights prior. Mad—no, Lilith—was good at covering her tracks. The dancing girl in pigtails from my previous visit cast a sly wink at me as she strutted by in a lace-corseted ensemble. Her body seemed to playfully bounce as she made her way over to her table to start dancing.

"What?" Wayne asked when I caught him also staring.

"Nothing," I said, bemused. I found it interesting vampires could blush.

"Where do you want to start looking? This place is packed."

I shook my head as we wove our way through the crowd, looking for any sign of Ronald. "Not sure. When I came here before, it was Lilith I encountered."

We reached a hallway on the far end of the casino floor, and I leaned back against the wall. Wayne snickered. Any remaining doubt I might have had he was related to Murray immediately dissipated as I examined the smugness of his expression.

"What?" I asked.

"You know that was a setup, right?"

"I do *now.*" I sighed. "At the time, I didn't know any better. She said she had been coming from rehearsal."

Wayne raised an eyebrow. "Seriously, in that costume?"

"Last I recalled, you weren't exactly complaining about it," I said.

I left the conversation there as we navigated our way through the crowd. If Wayne was going to give me this much shit over being stuck in an elevator with the woman, then I definitely needed to make sure I didn't let it slip I had slept with her.

A poster for *Illumination* hung on the wall in front of me. A placard with a large blue arrow hung underneath it.

"What do you think?" Wayne said, shifting his gaze from me to the poster.

I shrugged. "I say we follow the clues."

"Sounds good to me."

We followed the blue arrows down the hallway, to a set of ornately decorated doors made of polished white wood. I nodded to Wayne, and he pulled the doors open, revealing the showroom within. Rows of cushioned folding chairs separated by a walkway aisle sloped downward to a few feet in front of an orchestra pit. Behind the pit stood a large stage with red curtains that had been pulled back, revealing a series of silver-colored stairs and scaffolding comprising *Illumination*'s set design.

A man stood on the stage, facing us with his hands held behind his back. He wore a long black trench coat, and a matching set of shirt and pants, and black boots. *Not a man, not anymore.* We continued down the aisle. Nothing about Ronald had changed. His round face and goatee appeared the same as they had ten years ago.

"Ronald."

Wayne and I climbed a small set of stairs located near the apron of the stage. Ronald stood only ten feet away from us.

"Damn, Apollo." Ronald cocked his head to one side and sighed. "If you had taken any longer, I would've died all over again."

"What the fuck are you doing here?!" Dumb question, I know, but I needed to hear. I needed to know why he was involved in all of this.

"Can't I have a conversation with an old friend?" Ronald raised his hands palms up as he shrugged his shoulders.

"Not when the lives of others are at stake," I replied. "Enough with the pretense. Where are Murray and Dr. Griffin?"

Ronald rolled his eyes. "You're no fun," he said, mockingly sounding like a child who had just been scolded by his parents. "Fine. I'm working for Lilith, and I'm supposed to get you to trust me until she gets what she needs from the doctor."

Wayne leaned in close to me. "He's stalling, Apollo. I can hear heartbeats, two of them below us," he whispered, nodding toward the orchestra pit. I took a step in the indicated direction, but Ronald appeared right in front of me, blocking my path.

"Get the fuck out of my way, Ronald," I growled. I felt the uneasiness rising in my stomach. I didn't want to have to fight Ronald, but I knew it was inevitable. Ronald smiled wide, revealing his perfectly white vampire teeth.

Snap.

The sound coming from Ronald's fingers was all I heard before it went to shit. Two vampires, faces twisted and snarling, dropped out of the rafters, landing on the stage with a loud thud as Ronald thrust a fist forward. I don't know what hurt more—the punch connecting with the already swollen section of my face, or the fact its impact sent me flying backward off the apron of the stage, dropping six feet onto the floor. I had to roll to the side in order to keep from falling into the orchestra pit. I looked up just in time to see Wayne taking on the two vamps—right as Ronald landed next to me.

I managed to dodge out of the way, avoiding a kick to my gut. I got to my feet and spun around to block his incoming attack. He grabbed my arm, and twisted it behind my back, but not before I managed to pull out the stake I had hidden in my jacket. I heard a scream and would have jumped back if not for Ronald's grip.

The head of one of the vampires rolled in front of me, staring up at me with the pale whites of its eyes. This provided me enough of a distraction to elbow Ronald in the chest. He stumbled back just enough for me to break free. I spun around, stake held in front—then the head of the second vampire hit me in the face, knocking me over. Damn, that fucking hurt.

"Sorry!" Wayne yelled from the stage.

Never mind! I now knew what it felt like to be a bowling ball pin, and I had Ronald to deal with. Stars were still dancing in front of my face when Ronald lunged at me.

Fuck it. I was tired of this bullshit. Ronald had been my friend, but it was past time to end this. I stepped out of the way, and we exchanged a series of blows and punches. Wayne jumped down to assist. Being an older vampire, Wayne was slightly stronger than Ronald, and it didn't take him much effort before he had Ronald held by the arms with his chest facing toward me. I looked dejectedly at the stake in my hand, then back at Ronald. I knew what I had to do.

"You're an asshole," Ronald spat. The vampire's twisted face had nothing of the man I used to know.

"Do it!" Wayne shouted. "I can't hold him for much longer."

I was flooded with emotions, and nearly dropped to my knees. I had been mourning his loss for years. "Ronald, I'm sorry but—"

"The Ronald you knew is dead," Ronald spat again.

"I know." I closed my eyes, driving the stake into Ronald's heart. Watching him turn to dust, I sighed, "But I'm sorry."

12

"What's wrong?"

Wayne waved his hand in front of me as he relaxed his face, and I slowly came back to reality.

"I just killed one of my best friends who I thought was dead. What the fuck do you think?"

My body felt numb as I went through the motions of processing what had happened. Never mind once again, I had vampire dust on my jacket. I'm going to end up a dead man if I succeed in saving Murray's ass. Damned if you do, damned if you don't.

"I see." Wayne was smart not to say anything else. Not like the events that led to me running a stake through Ronald's heart were preventable.

I shook my head as I lowered my arm. "It doesn't make sense. Ronald never acted that way before." My grip on the stake held at my side remained tight.

Wayne shrugged as he walked past me. "Who knows? It could have been any number of things. Maybe it's because he's new as far as vampires are concerned, maybe it's because Lilith had him under her control. Maybe——"

"Ronald never acted that way when he was alive." I turned and glared at the back of Wayne's head.

"Okay, sorry," Wayne said, taking a step back. He jumped into the orchestra pit. The crashing sounds of chairs and music stands clanging together indicated his landing into the pit had not been entirely successful.

"What the hell are you doing?" I asked.

"I told you. I heard heartbeats," Wayne said. "In fact, I still hear them."

I regarded him curiously. "In the orchestra pit?"

"No, dumbass. Underneath." Wayne opened a narrow door in the pit below the stage. From where I stood, I could see a dimly lit hallway. "Are you coming, or do I need to save the world on my own?"

"Okay, okay, old man. No need to be so pushy," I said. My attempt at climbing down into the pit was barely a hair above successful. In fact, I'm fairly certain when the chair I lowered myself onto buckled beneath me, it made Wayne's entrance down here look downright graceful.

"At least you didn't land on your ass," Wayne said. He held the door open and smiled. I scowled and stormed past him, entering the hallway.

"Are you sure they are down here?" I asked. The hallway led us down a set of stairs, past a couple of music rehearsal rooms. Another door opened into a steel staircase, which unsurprisingly, led down.

Wayne tilted his head and sniffed. "Definitely. I can smell the blood, human blood." Something told me I didn't want to know how vampires differentiated blood types.

"Let's hurry," I said, rushing as quietly as possible

down the stairs. I worried about whatever potential harm might be occurring to Murray—and Dr. Griffin—but I also didn't want to alert whatever might be waiting for us. Knowing Lilith, she probably had this scenario planned all along. Fucking bitch.

We reached the bottom of the stairs, which opened into a stone corridor lit with evenly placed wall sconces casting an eerie glow. Thin steel pipes lined the ceiling. The pipes occasionally hissed as we walked past doors made of wood with steel bar windows. This place looked like a dungeon. Knowing Lilith, it probably was.

"Who the fuck owns enough money to build a place like this?" I wondered aloud.

"Lilith is old, Apollo. She's got more tricks up her sleeve than the pyramid of a Ponzi scheme. She could have done any number of things to earn the finances to have a place like this constructed." Wayne paused, looking at me with concern. "Apollo?"

I took a moment to steady myself. How old was Lilith, and how many people had she slept with before we fucked each other's brains out? *No, I don't want to know the answer.*

It wasn't long before I heard the echo of what sounded like a physical altercation. The dungeon hallway ended at a T intersection, on the left was another hallway, another series of doors lit by creepy lights. To the right, however, were a pair of female vampires dressed like Fifty-Shades-of-Undead guarding the door behind them. And from the looks of their vampire-mode faces, they were not entirely happy to see us.

"Something tells me Murray is in there."

"You mean the room being guarded by our domina-trix friends in the latex catsuits?" Wayne asked.

I nodded. I became immediately thankful I had the stake in my hand, or I would have been one dead Apollo when one of the vamps rushed at me. She got the pointy end of my stake in her heart and turned to dust immediately. Wayne dispatched the other one quickly, ripping off her head and tossing it to the floor. I stepped over the body of the headless vamp and walked toward Wayne, his face in vampire-mode.

When this was over, I would need to talk to Wayne about his anger management issues. He kicked the door in with his vamp strength, and it came off the hinges, shattering into pieces.

Murray sat chained to a wall, beaten to shit, looking worse than he did after we left Osiris Labs. Both of his eyes were now swollen shut. The vampire standing in front of him was the pig-tailed dancing girl I had seen up in the casino earlier. She didn't look as cute when she looked at me with her twisted vamp face, but hey, I'd probably hit it even if a paper bag was involved. Pig-Tails hissed at me, and I flung the stake at her. It whizzed past Wayne and lodged into her chest, but it must've missed her heart, because she didn't turn to dust or explode in a pile of blood and guts.

Wayne sped forward and broke the woman's neck before he savagely ripped off her head, tossing it carelessly. I sighed as her body slumped to the floor. She had such a cute ass.

"He's alive, thank goodness," Wayne said, relaxing his face back to its human form.

"Apollo…hurry…they took…doctor…" Murray wheezed as he lifted his head.

"Where?"

Murray pointed a finger down the hallway. Maybe he could see out of his eyes.

I looked at Wayne, who was having a horrible time trying to free Murray. "Go. Let me get him out of these chains, and I'll catch up," he said.

"Seriously? You can snap off vampire heads like opening a bottle of beer, but you can't get through some hardware store cast link chain—"

"Now, Apollo! The quicker we get to Lilith, the easier time we'll have in stopping her."

I sighed, and left both Murrays in the room, sprinting down the hallway, past the intersection we had arrived from. How the hell was I going to stop Lilith, someone who had the strength of multiple elder vampires, on my own?

I didn't have to race down the hallway long. It ended in a series of double doors, which swung inward to reveal a room which appeared in sharp contrast to the rest of Lilith's underground complex.

It felt like I had stepped through a portal into an alternate reality. The room before me looked clean and immaculate. A desk with computer on it stood along one wall, and a series of tables with various glass containers containing liquids of all different colors sat in neat, little rows.

A man of my height, wearing a lab coat, stood at the far end of the room. He paid me no heed as I approached. I had barely made it within a few steps of him when he stopped and turned to face me, pushing his glasses up his nose. Slightly balding, thin greying hair—there was no mistaking the man in front of me for anyone other than Dr. Clarence Griffin. In one hand, he held a glass beaker with a clear liquid. A tiny wisp of smoke wafted through the container's opening.

The doctor furrowed his brow as he regarded my presence.

"Do you mind? You're in my way. I need to finish this." He pushed past me and walked over to a table with a set of empty collection vials sitting in a tray.

Why did I feel like I just wasted all my time bungling a rescue?

I spun around to face the man. "I don't have time for this, Dr.—"

"Stop, don't interrupt." he shouted. "If I don't complete this, they'll kill my son!"

What kind of games is he playing at? Surely, he would have known about Connor. Something about the man's demeanor didn't feel right.

"Your son is already dead," I said.

Dr. Griffin paused for a moment, looked at me and shrugged as if I told him water was wet. He immediately went back to work, muttering to himself as he poured liquid from the vial into another.

What the fucking hell…

Lilith. She had him under her control. I wasn't about to investigate the man's body for elder vampire scratches.

"It is finished, but only enough for one." Dr. Griffin smiled as he held up a collection vial, containing a small amount of blue liquid, closing the cap before placing it in the tray.

"Dr. Griffin, I need to get you out of here. It's dangerous. Let's go. You're coming with me." I grabbed his arm and started leading him toward the exit.

The doctor shook his head and pulled away from my grip. I furrowed my brow. "You don't understand. It's too late," he said.

"What are you talking about?" I barely noticed his gaze shift past my shoulder.

You know that blood-curdling feeling you get when everything goes dead silent? I didn't have to guess who stood behind me when I heard the double doors to the lab open. I recognized the sweet, melodic voice immediately.

"Hello, Apollo." Lilith whispered into my ear.

"Lilith."

"Apollo."

"I liked you better when you were wearing flower print underwear," I said dryly.

Lilith slinked around to face me. My cheek warmed as I clenched my jaw. She had her raven-black hair pulled back in a tight braid and wore a leather corset and pants that almost seemed to have been painted over her curves.

Lilith held a hand in front of her face as she laughed. "As I recall, you liked it when I wasn't wearing anything."

"Whatever," I said. I tried desperately not to stare at her backside as she strutted away, but I failed. Miserably. Fucking tease.

"I suppose I should be thanking you. Assisting me with getting Connor killed provided the good doctor here the right kind of motivation to repeat the act of kindness he showed me. Speaking of which, darling," Lilith said, taking the blue vial out of Dr. Griffin's hand. "I need you to get back to work and make more of this wonderful concoction."

Dr. Griffin nodded, and walked over to the back of

the room.

"I can't let you do that." I grabbed her wrist. The vial dropped to the floor and rolled away.

"Are you sure?" Lilith asked. "I can be pretty convincing."

She smiled and took a step forward. Even without the scratch marks, I would have been entranced by the beauty of the woman before me. Before I could react, Lilith had me pressed against one of the tables, one hand behind my neck, and kissed me passionately. It's kind of hard to resist when a woman has you by the balls. I mean that literally. Her other hand found its way inside my pants, and damn, whatever she was doing felt good.

Much to my own surprise and regret, I removed Lilith's hand from my manhood and pushed her away.

"Not gonna work this time," I said. From the sweat pooling at the back of my neck, if she pulled that trick again, I knew it would be game over.

"You know, I could've made you like me, and used the cure to take the blood lust away," she said. Her voice was like honey, and I was pretty sure she'd trapped more than one fly in its sweet nectar of goodness.

Movement from the corner of my eye caught my attention. Whatever Wayne was planning to do, I needed to keep up the distraction. Not an incredibly difficult task. I wasn't exactly offended by Lilith's presence or flirtations.

"I'd rather live the one life," I said. "I've seen what being a vampire did to Ronald, and I'd rather not end up like that."

"I thought you would appreciate me affording you the opportunity to have a reunion."

"Why, Lilith? Why go through all the trouble?"

Lilith shrugged. "I was bored,"

Okay, now that pissed me off. "You're telling me you're trying to create an army of super vampires, and have been spending the past decade screwing with me, because you're bored?"

"Essentially," she said. "When you've lived as long as I have, you have to keep yourself entertained. I needed a new hobby."

Fucking she-demon.

"Destroy whatever is on the computer!" Wayne shouted as he lunged at Lilith. She spun, kicking him in the stomach, and sent him flying into the wall. He reached for something near his side when he landed on the floor. The vial containing the cure.

"Break the damn thing!"

Instead, Wayne uncorked the vial and drank it in one gulp.

"Madison?!" Murray exclaimed, rushing toward the computer station. The swelling in his face had gone down. He looked around with both eyes, even though he was beat to shit. Wayne must have used vampire blood to heal him.

"Don't worry. He won't turn." Wayne looked at me. "I only gave him enough of my blood to heal, and I'm not going to drink from the veins of my own grandson. That would just be weird."

I didn't have time to ask any questions or give Wayne a piece of my mind for drinking the only known cure, because Lilith jumped on top of me, pinning me to the floor, and not in the fun way.

Or maybe it was the fun way. I mean, rolling around on the floor engaged in a physical altercation with a hot Vegas showgirl who has a fantastic ass doesn't leave much for a person like me to complain about. Eventually, I landed on top and pinned her to the ground. For the first time, I saw Lilith's vampire visage. Yeah, not so cute.

"Your face needs some work," I said.

"Fuck you, Apollo," she spat.

"Been there, done that—"

"Apollo Grant, what the hell is she talking about?" Murray raised an eyebrow at me.

"We'll talk later!" I said.

I've known for a while vampires were capable of moving fast, but this woman was nothing short of a Category 5 hurricane on steroids. We are talking about someone who performed in a Vegas stage show twelve times a week in six-inch stiletto heels while wearing angel wings that weighed like a tank. Never mind she's an elder vampire.

Lilith being a denizen of hell, was definitely no angel. Screaming, I punched her in the face before she flung me off. Somehow, I managed to knock her out. I wanted to stake her cold black heart. Reaching inside my jacket, I immediately regretted leaving the weapon behind in the room where Murray had previously been held captive.

"Fuck it! I can't get the files to erase!" Murray shouted.

"Here, let me help," Dr. Griffin said, running toward Murray.

A *pop* sounded from behind as I clocked Lilith square in the jaw one more time for good measure. Dr. Griffin had poured liquid over the computer, setting the equipment on fire.

The flames started to spread.

The last thing I saw as Wayne dragged me out of the lab was Lilith lying unconscious on the floor.

13

Wayne and I sat on the roof of the Queen's Pawn and watched the smoke rise from what used to be the Phoenix off in the distance. The sun had risen moments prior, and even though I knew he had drunk the cure, the vampire sitting next to me did not light up like a firework. I both looked and felt like shit and refused Wayne's offer of some of his blood to heal. It sounded gross to begin with. We didn't know what the cure did exactly to the blood-curse, and I wanted to feel the pain of my injuries.

"You think she died in the fire?" Wayne asked, leaning back in his folding chair. He held a can of cheap beer in his hand.

"Fuck no, that devil woman is persistent, but I doubt we'll see her anytime soon." I took a swig from my own can of the swill. I doubted even if I had time to find my stake, run back and stab Lilith, she'd stay dead.

Wayne took another drink. "Think she's pissed?"

"I'd be surprised if she wasn't." I laughed.

"Reggie?"

I sighed. "Murray will get over it. We've been through worse."

"I meant is he finished with the doctor?" Wayne asked.

"Aren't you supposed to be helping him?" I took the last sip of my can before crushing it and tossing it back onto the roof. After our escape from the Phoenix, Murray went straight to work crafting a new identity for Dr. Griffin.

Wayne shrugged. "He seems to have that situation under control for the time being. I don't want to get in his way. He's perfectly capable of destroying all of her records and wiping her bank accounts while he gets the doctor squared away. Mentioned something about making a generous donation in her name to the Red Cross," he snickered before continuing, "Besides, you're not the only one he's refusing to speak with."

Murray wasn't thrilled Wayne had drunk the vial containing the blood-curse cure. And he definitely hadn't been thrilled with me for sleeping with his girlfriend. I had a freshly busted lip to prove it, but it was difficult to tell given how badly I had been beat to shit over the past thirty-six hours. At least the elder vampire marks on the side of my neck had faded away.

"What are you going to do now, Wayne?" I asked.

"I have no idea." Wayne said. "Maybe go drink a few beers, ride off into the sunset. This is weird. I feel like a vampire, but the bloodlust is gone. There has to be more to that vial than what we know. As much as I'm enjoying the warmth of the sun on my skin, I should be burnt to ash by now."

"You'll need to be careful," I cautioned. "Lilith might come after you next."

Wayne chugged the rest of his beer, then set the can

on the edge of the roof railing. He let out a belch I'm fairly certain only vampires could pull from the pits of hell. "Enough about me, you plan on sticking around?" he asked.

"The apartment?"

Wayne scowled. "No, dipshit. Vegas"

"To be honest, I don't know," I said. "Ronald was the reason I came here, and now he's dead. For real this time. Murray's pissed I slept with Lilith, and I have this odd feeling I'm nowhere close to being done with her yet. I wish there had been time enough to stake her."

The sound of rusted metal grated as the access door to the roof opened from behind us. Murray stepped out; his face healed. He had also changed his clothes to much cleaner attire, consisting of a torn T-shirt and jeans. His appearance reminded me the leather jacket I wore was covered in vampire blood and dust.

"Murray?" I asked.

"Don't think because I'm here, I'm done being upset with you," Murray said. "We need to talk."

"Hey man, if it's about Lil—"

Murray raised a hand. "Shut up for a sec, will you, Apollo? Given how much crap she put us both through I shouldn't hate you, but you did bang my girlfriend so—"

I instinctively raised a hand to my busted lip, fully expecting another ass-kicking from my roommate.

"Reggie," Wayne cautioned.

"Grandpa, don't call me that. Not now." Murray's voice remained stern, but the worry in his tone revealed he didn't intend on coming up here to instigate another argument about Lilith or the mess stuck to my jacket.

"What's going on?" I asked.

"Tal called. Says she's got another client for us. They paid in advance," Murray said.

"Since when did Tal become a booker? Norman usually assigns our gigs," I replied. Curious, but…money was money.

Murray shook his head. "That's just it. Norman's gone missing"

Wayne and I exchanged confused glances at each other and sighed. Well shit, here we go again. Hopefully, it doesn't involve blackjack and hookers.

THE END

ABOUT REY NICHOLS

Rey Nichols is a writer from North Carolina who specializes in urban fantasy, sci-fi noir, and supernatural horror. She often spends her days drinking hot cocoa and is a board game aficionado. She plays a mean game of Carcassonne and has an unhealthy addiction with Eldritch Horror. Rey has several works in progress, which you can learn about by visiting her website at http://www.reynichols.com.

Made in the USA
Columbia, SC
18 August 2022

64871532R00076